AF651940

Contents

On the Edge 7

The Trap 44

The Curse 51

Black Beads and Television 76

Toilets 86

Childhood 129

Atonement 139

The Orbit of Confusion 148

Translator's Note 189

On the Edge

Their journey, finalized after weeks of planning, is about to begin. She is standing in the passage near the back entrance, putting on her burqa as she chats with her mother.

'My precious child, I wonder how Allah gave you so much patience! May you live a hundred years,' Amma's eyes grow moist as she blesses her daughter.

'Why say all this, Amma?' she demurs.

'Well, is it easy to look after these old hags? It's my responsibility, but *you* are bearing the brunt. Couldn't Allah have given me the patience he has given you? I get angry even before I get up in the morning, don't I?' Amma sits down on the grinding stone placed near the back entrance.

'Of course you get angry! But you end up showing your anger at the wrong person, don't you?' The sting in her tone must have upset Amma. Like a touch-me-not plant, her face falls instantly.

Amma is desperate to make her daughter understand her perspective, and the anxiety is clear on her face. Pretending to wipe it with the end of her sari, she says, 'What do you want me to do? Can't you see what the old woman is up to?'

'Why just grandmother? Why don't you show your anger with him?…You only follow him around, carrying his spittoon…' Then realizing the unmistakable rancour in her words, she calms down.

How foolish of me! Scolding herself, she turns to her mother and says, 'All right, leave it. I was only teasing you. I'll be going, then?' She steps out of the house with a smile on her face, but casts a nervous glance behind to check if her mother is following.

The car is parked in front of the house under the early morning sun. Nanni is waiting next to it, her bag of pills wedged in the crook of her armpit. Not realizing that Nanni has been waiting only for her, she says, 'Um, get in quick…it's really hot today.' She wonders if the voice dripping with concern is really hers. How did her voice, which had sounded so severe with her mother just minutes ago, acquire this fawning lilt? She starts to feel guilty about the way she has behaved with her mother.

Feeling a pang of melancholy, she reaches for the passenger door. Just when she is about to get in, Nanni's command makes her pause: 'You come and sit here. I'll get in after you.' She collects herself. Unable to make sense of her intervention, she peers intently at Nanni's face, giving her an inquiring look. Nanni's old face, fraught with anxiety, demands that she instantly comply with her wish.

Unwilling to accept Nanni's authority, she mutters, 'Why, the front seat is vacant.'

'Cha. Come here, I'm telling you!' Nanni rebukes her, sounding put out.

Considering Nanni's needlessly harsh tone, she offers no reply. Slamming the front door shut, she moves to the back and sits next to Raadhi, who is already inside. As though she has been waiting only for Jassi to get in, Nanni climbs in quickly to sit beside her. Nanni's face wears a triumphant smile. Though she realizes, in the shadow of that smile, the tangle she is caught up in, she ignores it because this situation is so familiar.

Chacha, who is standing in a corner of the veranda and waiting for them to get on board, says, 'Shall we start, then?' Without waiting for a reply, he gets into the driver's seat and starts the car. She is hurt that Amma hasn't come outside to see them off. That her words could have wounded Amma makes her despondent.

The car races steadily over the smooth tarmac. Feeling very uncomfortable in her perch between Raadhi and Nanni, she gazes wistfully at the empty seat in the front.

Raadhi is very obese. Sitting with her swollen legs splayed, she occupies half the backseat. Squeezed between the two women, she begins to seriously worry about how she is going to manage them both through a whole day.

Though she is aware of the problems involved in taking both of them anywhere together, it is her fault that she did not foresee just how bad it could get. She begins to reproach herself. Thinking of herself as a mouse caught in a trap is not pleasant at all.

Yesterday, as soon as the plan for the trip was finalized, Nanni had warned her privately: 'Look here. Don't let that woman babble endlessly inside the car. And then you must never let her sit next to me. Her whole body stinks because she never bathes...and never put on the air-conditioner. That woman will keep farting. If you keep the windows rolled up, the stink will make my stomach turn.'

Such grave concerns! The thought of how much time Nanni must have spent worrying about such things pained her even more. However, since she was well aware of Nanni's special traits, her warnings didn't seem particularly odd.

It is a miracle if Raadhi bathes more than twice a week. She believes that a person is sure to catch a cold if they bathe often. All efforts by everyone at home to dispel this belief have proved futile.

Nanni, however, is her exact opposite. She can make anyone who is around her for a day feel extremely unclean. None of them could bear to watch the horror of her spending three-quarters of every day in the bathroom. Whenever she got fed up, Raadhi would whine to her: 'If I ever wasted water like this, your mother would shoot me dead. That's just my bad luck.'

It was true, though. Nanni's activities could be a source of great distress for onlookers. She needed half an hour just to clean her teeth and wash her face in the morning, another two and a half hours if she started bathing at nine, and an hour for her ablutions before each prayer of the day.

Over the past few years, all her time was spent this way, in the company of water. When she hinted once to Nanni about consulting a doctor, Nanni told her: 'Why, do you think I am crazy? I won't do it. If you like, take your Raadhi and show her to a doctor for lunatics.'

Every time she sees Nanni come out of the bathroom, she is seized with wonder. Nanni does glance at the clock before entering, but how does she keep track of the time for her exit? How is she able to manage it so precisely each time?

While in the bathroom, Nanni is used to keeping the door ajar, never fully closing it. When she is bathing, people moving about outside can get a good look at her. Nanni is not bothered about it in the least.

To Amma who had once muttered, 'Why can't you close the door and bolt it from inside?' Nanni replied with disdain, 'Why should I? Won't I feel suffocated? Who is going to turn up here, near the rear entrance?'

It had been her long-time wish to watch Nanni from outside while she was taking a bath. But since she didn't have the requisite patience, she thought she could at least watch her perform *Olu.* So, one day she sat down on the grinding stone in front of the bathroom door, a bunch of loose flowers in her lap, well before Nanni was expected to arrive. The late afternoon sun was drifting down the wall in the backyard.

Nanni arrives exactly at four to enter the bathroom. When she sees Jassi sitting there, which is quite unusual, she offers a faint smile. 'I am going to perform *Olu* for *Asar*,' she says as she shuts the door, leaving it just a little ajar. Even the angle at which she leaves it ajar is always the same. Nanni brushes her teeth once before the *Asar* prayer.

Stringing the flowers on her lap, she casts a furtive look around. After the water flows noisily and fills the bucket, Nanni upends it suddenly to let it all out. She guesses that Nanni has cleaned the bucket. Then water from the tap begins to fill the bucket again. When Nanni squats on her haunches to pee, she can see her bare bottom through the half-open door. She lowers her head in embarrassment.

The sound of the water is turning into unrelenting noise. As Nanni begins to scoop water with a mug again and again to pour it between her thighs and wash herself, she begins to count. One, two, three… Nanni is indefatigable…fifty-eight, fifty-nine, sixty…At last, Nanni stands up.

Again, she hears the sound of the plastic mug colliding against the steel bucket. Nanni begins to perform *Olu*. She hears Nanni scooping water and slapping it on her face and hands. The sound of clinking bangles confirms that she is scrubbing her hands very hard. As she begins to wonder how Nanni's body could have so much filth to warrant all that scrubbing, she is filled with compassion for her instead of anger. Her heart overflows with boundless love for this woman, who spends most of her hours inside the bathroom, every single day. The sound of water flowing from the bathroom is relentless.

Loose jasmine flowers are wilting between her fingers. When Nanni comes out, her face is slack, like an overripe fruit. Smiling placidly at her, Nanni walks towards her room. Planting her pale, water-soaked feet gently on the floor, she walks delicately, like a sauntering bird. At all times, Nanni's room admits no one but her. She has never seen anyone being allowed entry into that room. She recalls how anxious Nanni had been, uncertain whether to welcome her or turn her away, when she had deliberately barged into her room one day.

'Come, Jassi,' Nanni greeted her half-heartedly, 'sit on this chair.' She pushed a wire-knit chair hastily in front. Her voice betrayed the anxiety that the visitor must not sit on her mattress.

It is the smallest room in the house. A bed, cupboard and chair; the only free space left is sufficient for spreading her prayer mat. The washing line is tied between the iron ring above the bed and the window bar overhead. Several scraps of a torn voile sari have been rolled up and inserted into the gaps between the window bars. She knows that each rag is meant for a special purpose: one for nose cleaning, another for scrubbing ears, yet another for wiping hands, and still one more solely for foot cleaning. Each rag is stuffed into a different gap.

Though it's been over five years since the house was built, the walls and the floor sparkle as though it was finished only yesterday. Nanni, who meets her eye uneasily, is growing more and more restive and anxious. As one edge of the thin cotton towel hanging over her head sways in the breeze from the fan, Nanni moves forward urgently, her face full of worry that it might graze her visitor's head, pushes it to the far end of the line and smiles at her.

In order to seem oblivious to Nanni's predicament, she casts a quick glance around the room, surveying its orderly arrangements.

Unable to grasp the meaning of her glance, Nanni says, 'Why are you looking around as though it's something new? This is your house.' She laughs, exposing most of her betel-stained teeth. Even so, Nanni's gaze is directed at her feet which are planted firmly on the floor. After peering at them nervously, worried that they might be filthy, Nanni is soaked in the distress of being unable to reach a firm conclusion.

Reflecting on the way Nanni seems to be waiting for her to leave the room and how, in the space of a couple of minutes, she has made her feel like a filthy tramp, Jassi is not sure whether what she now feels for Nanni is pity or anger. Emerging out of a long silence, she mumbles, 'Why, is it a problem if I look around?' in an attempt to ease the tension.

'Why not? Look around all you want. It's your house, after all,' Nanni says, and sits on the bed. From the dainty way she sits, it seems as though she is afraid she might hurt the bed. The whiteness of the bedcover, which has been spread without a single wrinkle, is intended to please the heart. The monthly magazine *Nargis* is lying open and face down in the middle of the bed. While Raadhi doesn't like to read, Nanni reads voraciously. Along with several religious publications, she reads weekly magazines like *Rani* and *Kalkandu*, as well as children's books—not leaving anything out.

Her gaze falls on the sheet of paper spread next to the pillow, and the bit of cloth folded and placed on it. As she stares intently at the cloth, wondering why it has been kept there, Nanni volunteers an explanation: 'That bit is for wiping sweat. I didn't want to keep it on the bed, so I've put it on the paper. The sheet will get dirty, no?'

Lacking the fortitude to stay there any longer, she comes out of the room. Her younger brother rebuked her that evening: 'Why would you do such a thing? After you left the room, did you see how she poured water over the chair you sat on and washed it for an hour? Do any of us enter that room? Why do you go there and humiliate yourself?'

She is terribly hurt by his remarks. The next day she goes to her mother as she is cutting vegetables in the kitchen and says, 'Amma, we have to show her to a doctor. How shall we do it?'

'What do I know about such things? Take care of the whole mess yourself. Because of this woman, we get an electricity bill of a thousand rupees every month. As if this is not trouble enough, that old woman Raadhi doesn't bathe even once a week. She stinks up the place. It's my wretched fate. On top of that, there's the antics of your Raadhi the moment this woman enters the bathroom, whining every five minutes, "Allah, I badly need to pee, what can I do?" She will pace up and down between the bathroom and the hall, sucking my life out in the process. Half the time, they seem to do this deliberately.' Amma's agony is heart-rending.

Freed from her memories, she notes the trees rushing swiftly past the open window and the wind blowing steadily on her face. Fed up of pushing away the hair falling across her face, she worries that when they reach home it will all be a mess. Making up her mind, she says, 'Roll up the windows and turn on the AC, Chacha.'

'What did you say—turn on the AC?' As he turns his head back to ask her, Chacha sees her plight and his face shrinks in dismay.

'Why are you sitting cramped up when the front seat is empty?' he says.

'No, it's quite comfortable here,' as she declines hastily, she wishes that there was at least some justification for her refusal.

Out of the corner of her eye, she notices Nanni's displeasure at her request for the AC, contrary to her prior instructions, and laughs inwardly.

As Raadhi starts enjoying the chill of the AC within minutes, Nanni is lost in thought. Because she knows that Nanni's thinking is unlikely to be on the right track, she says by way of underlining the need for the AC, 'The sun is really hot today, isn't it? It's late October, but the heat is so punishing.'

Because she doesn't know whom to address, she says it to no one in particular.

The moment her voice fades, Raadhi, who has remained silent all this while, quickly opens her eyes and says, 'Yes, yes. The times are bad. When it should rain and when the sun should shine…all these calculations have changed. Everything has turned topsy-turvy. Maybe the time of qayamat is nearing. How that wretched sun is tormenting this poor old woman!'

Like a torrential waterfall, Raadhi's words flood the car's interior. She is seized by the need to do something to stop her. Though she wants to check the change of expression in Nanni's old, oblong face, she is not brave enough to face her directly; so she tries to bear Raadhi's grumbling with equanimity. Again, she remembers her mother.

She wonders if she has been too harsh to her mother that morning. Poor thing, how can Amma express her anger to her husband? Won't it be a sin before Allah? That's why she takes her anger out on other people. Most of her rages are directed at Raadhi, and for valid reasons.

From as far back as she could remember, Father always came home to eat right after the *luha* prayer. The moment he entered the house, he would ask, 'Is the food ready?' Amma would be rushing between the hall and the kitchen at that time. She would run around like a child, getting ready to serve the food. On some days, the kerosene stove would not light. At those times, she would look plaintively at her husband, who had already started eating in haste, and plead, 'Please. Why don't you eat a little slowly? The eggs are still cooking.'

Just when he, too, was about to accept her plea, Raadhi would intervene and complain: 'Shouldn't a woman be mindful of when a man is expected home? She doesn't keep the food ready, that's how much she cares!'

That would be it. Father would take his plate piled with food and toss it deftly down the hall. 'A woman should have some fear in her!' Gnashing his teeth, he would march out of the house. Amma would run after him up to the pyol on the front veranda, pleading, and then come back inside, disappointed. After that, her entire fury would turn on Raadhi.

'Old, widowed hag! You've chased the man out of his house without letting him eat in peace. May you stay well and fill your wretched belly.'

'What did I do? Did I ask him not to eat?' Raadhi would start whining.

As the burden of memories becomes unbearable, she opens her eyes and glances at her watch. They must travel another two hours at least. She feels weary. Since they have an appointment with the doctor, they won't have to wait. But she becomes increasingly anxious that they should reach home without encountering any major problem on the way. The minutes are crawling by. She has an idea: shall we go a little faster? She wonders nervously what obstacle might crop up before they try.

Suddenly, Nanni's index finger jabs at her waist from the right. Collecting herself, she turns to face Nanni. 'What do you want?'

'Won't you ask him to turn off the AC?' After hissing secretively in her ear so Radhi can't hear, Nanni jabs her waist again twice without waiting for a reply.

Hastily, she turns towards Raadhi. Raadhi is reclining with her eyes closed. She turns back towards Nanni and silences her with her eyes. 'Chacha, we've had enough of the AC. Please turn it off. We can keep the windows open for some time.'

Jassi starts praying to God that Raadhi should not come to know that this has happened by Nanni's wish. Chacha must have been confused by her request. He turns and looks at her, as if to ask why she has changed her mind after having complained earlier about the heat. Without a word, he turns off the AC and rolls down the windows.

Resolving that she must never turn in Raadhi's direction, not even by accident, she closes her eyes tight and leans back in her seat.

'Taking both of them together in the same car will be very difficult. If you take them separately, it would double the expense. Unnecessary travel, too.' Amma's admonition sounds in her ears.

'Uss…the pain is unbearable. What time are we supposed to meet the doctor?' Raadhi asks, splaying her swollen legs wider for comfort. 'Go a little faster…my stomach is heaving and the pain in my leg is squeezing the life out of me,' Raadhi complains to her son.

Chacha, who empathizes with her condition, steps on the accelerator. His reflection in the rear-view mirror makes her realize that he is deeply worried.

For the past few days, Raadhi has been unable to pass urine. She also vomited throughout the previous night. Not just her legs, but her whole body has become somewhat stiff. Her bloated belly is not a pretty sight.

As the car speeds up, it brings the wind's fury

inside, dislodging the covering from Raadhi's and Nanni's heads. Whereas Raadhi does not seem to mind, Nanni's hands are constantly busy straightening her head cover. What could happen if she left her head uncovered for some time? she wonders idly, and turns to watch the road. The tarmac glistens in the heat of the midday sun. At a higher speed, the car fills up with hot wind. The trees, drenched in the sun, stand in silent rows, heads bowed along both sides of the road. On one side, the mirage is shimmering like water on the rocks visible in the distance. Though she wants to go over the day's tasks, she realizes that it would be pointless and drops the idea.

She is extremely annoyed when Nanni's index finger jabs her waist again. She turns to her. 'What's the matter?'

'Tell him not to go so fast,' Nanni whispers in her ear. Anger glows inside her like a burning ember. How does the car's speed matter? It is because Raadhi can't travel for long hours with her swollen legs that they are going fast. So, why does it bother this old woman? For a moment, she thinks of silencing Nanni with a sharp word, but she buries the rage deep within herself. If she uttered a hasty word in anger, then how would she cope with the consequences? The thought calms her.

A wrong word from Amma on some rare occasion was enough for Nanni.

'Yes, I have no one to take care of me and I've have taken shelter in your house. That's why I must put up with this abuse. Allah, won't you take this cursed head back unto yourself?' Nanni would keep whining in several registers till she was exhausted.

'Such bravado when you are staying in your nephew's house,' Amma would moan. Knowing that Nanni was already feeling humiliated by having to seek refuge in her nephew's house, and that Amma must not wound Nanni further, she would shush her mother.

Raadhi starts grumbling about the pain in her legs. The way she keeps punctuating her story with, 'Do you know what I am saying?' seems to be an attempt on her part to affirm that she is not whining entirely to herself.

When Nanni's fingertip jabs her waist again, she responds nonchalantly, asking what has been bothering her. Nanni's slack face is red with anger. Without parting her thick, dry lips, she says, 'Ask him to play songs.' The harshness in her tone is new. It is a ploy to indicate that her request was intended to stop Raadhi's whining. But she knows that Nanni is very fond of listening to music, especially songs.

'Chacha, why don't you play some songs? I am getting bored,' she says casually, gazing at the trees lining both sides of the road. He must have wanted this too. As if he has been waiting only for her request, a song starts the very next moment. Sweeping away the cacophony of speech that has filled it thus far, music begins to flood through the car.

Even though she doesn't care much for the song, it is the only way to stop Raadhi's relentless grumbling. Because of the jerks caused by the road's uneven surface, she is toppling, by turns, on Nanni and Raadhi. Whenever she falls on Nanni, the old woman's ordeal makes her giggle. She wonders how hard Nanni's sari might be beaten the next day and laughs inwardly. A sari that normally received three hundred strokes on the washing stone is going to get, for grazing her and touching the hospital chair, two hundred more strokes she reckons.

'What kind of dirt could be there on that sari? Why should a woman who mostly keeps to herself in her room act so deranged? One sari is worn to tatters every month. Look how she is gnashing her teeth when she beats that sari.' Amma's habitual lament pops up in her mind.

Ponni always refused to wash Nanni's ambar

sari. 'I don't have the strength to beat it two hundred times, Amma,' she said. Nanni has retained some other woman exclusively for washing her saris. At twenty rupees per sari, with a precise count of the number of times each side should be slapped on the stone. As soon as the servant starts washing, Nanni stands a little away and starts counting. After beating the sari a hundred times on one side and another hundred on the other, so hard each time that the house itself shakes, the girl stops, panting for breath, her body drenched in sweat. After her departure, Nanni continues as best as she can with the remaining strokes. Her panting robs everyone at home of their peace. She fills the big bucket with water thirty times to rinse her sari over and over again, emptying the bucket on the floor each time and watching the water drain away.

That Nanni's slender frame proves equal to all that labour always surprised her.

While Nanni is at it near the entrance, Raadhi would hobble all the way there with her slow gait, her fat body swaying gently with each step, and observe the scene before disappearing into her room.

Although it had become a daily spectacle, it did trouble everyone in the house in some way.

'Girl, how long will it take to reach?' As she comes back to reality upon hearing Raadhi's voice, she raises her left wrist to check her watch. 'A few more hours to go,' she replies wearily, and tries to lose herself in the sweetness of the melody. She feels her heart grow light and wonders how music seems to have, more than anything else, such power to influence moods. As she reclines in her seat again and closes her eyes, she is further pleased that Raadhi has stopped her whining.

When a finger jabs her again in the waist, she is really annoyed and the displeasure creases her face. She firmly asks Nanni what is troubling her.

Nanni's face wears a tranquil expression. She feels like dropping all her grievances against her that very minute. Nanni brings her ripe old face close to her ear. She tries to guess what Nanni might have to say this time.

'The song that got over just now? Tell him to play it again,' she whispers very faintly, cravenly, in her ear. Her face is flushed with shame and embarrassment.

Which song? What is she saying? Unable to understand immediately, she collects her thoughts and then remembers the song Nanni has requested. The reason for Nanni's embarrassment: it is a love song.

Pretending not to notice her embarrassment, she says casually, 'Oh, you want that one...' and then adds, 'I like that song, too.' Her voice is even more subdued than Nanni's.

'Don't let on that I asked for it,' Nanni mutters nervously.

As she nods to reassure Nanni, her earnest expression quells the old woman's anxiety.

She casts a sidelong glance at Raadhi to find out where her attention is focused. Having stopped her whining, Raadhi is reclining with her eyes closed. The hot wind blows past her fat, ruddy cheeks.

'Chacha, you know the song which played just now? Play it again. It's a fine song.' Her voice falters in embarrassment. The awkwardness of requesting one's own uncle to play a love song is rather novel.

'Which song?' Turning back to look at her, he doesn't wait for an answer before rewinding the cassette to the previous track. As the song starts again, she senses the tremors it sets off in Raadhi's body, a warning that the old woman is quite awake and attentive even though her eyes are closed.

Raadhi knows about Nanni's obsessive need for music. Since it is certain now that Raadhi might interfere, she is determined not to allow it. As a defense, she starts to visibly enjoy the song. She taps the fingers of her left hand on her thigh, exaggerating her pleasure in the melody. Even though she herself finds this somewhat excessive, she continues her pretence—having no other option—and waits for the song's climax.

Even as she is bracing to heave a sigh of relief at the end, Nanni's finger, which pokes her waist at an unexpected moment, brings on a feeling of profound weariness. She stares angrily at her as if to ask: So, what *more* do you want now? Oblivious to the cinders burning in her eyes, Nanni pleads silently with her eyes for the same song to be played again.

As she tries to ignore Nanni's pinches, she is troubled by the abject pleading in her eyes. 'Allah, won't we reach there soon!' she groans to herself. Looking over at Nanni's face as if to confirm this would indeed be the last time, she turns immediately and says, 'Play the same song again, let's hear it.' Although saying it quickly obliterates the interval between thinking and utterance, her throat shrivels up in shame. Quickly, she grabs the bottle lying by her feet and pours some water down her mouth.

She senses a kind of languor in Chacha's driving. The smile he wears on his face is totally strange. She is anxious to convince him that she is the one who likes that song. But since she doesn't know how to tell him, she falls silent and begins to steal glances at Raadhi. When the song is played for the third time, Raadhi shakes off her drowsiness and, turning her fat body towards Nanni, begins to watch her closely.

Flushed with the sweetness of the melody and the pleasure of triumph, Nanni is reclining elegantly in her seat. The conceit of orchestrating everything as per her wishes has softened her features. Looking at Nanni, she is able to see why Raadhi's expression has suddenly turned grim. As if in an unseemly hurry to wipe that pride off Nanni's face and disparage her, Raadhi begins:

'Won't you stop that rubbish? Is this what we are supposed to listen to when we are travelling? Why don't you play a cassette of prayer songs to Allah, so he may lighten our journey, instead of making us listen to nonsense endearments such as doe and honey?' She scowls, contorting her features, and looks disgusted. Beyond the tone of mockery directed at Nanni, a note of authority—this is her son's car—is predominant in her voice.

It pains her to watch Nanni's face, which has shrunk in humiliation. She is bewildered, not knowing what to do. 'Stop that rubbish,' Raadhi's voice commands again. The command is enough to frighten not only Nanni but her as well.

Though he senses the sudden tension inside the car, Chacha holds his peace. Slowing down, he picks out the cassette of prayer songs and inserts it into the player. Nanni's face, which has darkened with the humiliation of defeat, looks irreparably damaged. The hurt from having her wishes denied and the grief of having her powerlessness affirmed combine to make her look extremely dejected.

Raadhi enjoys the devotional song as soon as it starts playing, as if savouring a personal victory. Intent on showing off her keen involvement to her granddaughter, Raadhi says, 'Ei, what a fine voice—hear that?' with a note of elation. While Raadhi's exaggerated admiration of the song continues to irritate her, the car is eating up the road's black top as it glides forward. As the despondency created by the skirmishes inside the car is nearing a peak, she feels an immeasurable annoyance well up inside, threatening to drown her. She is further aggravated by the devotional song, but she can hardly ignore it. Feeling perplexed, she grits her teeth and swallows her anger. The winding road makes them feel as if they are looking for their destination after having lost sight of it.

With her eyes closed and head swaying from side to side, Raadhi has a firm notion that she is doing something appropriate for her age and it makes her look pious and noble. Her behaviour seems to repudiate and mock Nanni's craving for music.

The long corridor at the hospital, teeming with patients, depresses her even more. With the smell of antiseptic assaulting her nose, she walks ahead to look for a seat, followed closely by Nanni and Raadhi. Spotting a few empty chairs along the wall adjoining the doctor's room, she hurries towards them. 'Hold my hand,' Raadhi calls out to her as she moves her swollen legs with great difficulty.

She goes back to Raadhi, puts an arm around her and leads her to a chair. Nanni, with her bag of pills tucked under an elbow, walks towards them with a steady and dignified gait. Her face proudly proclaims to Raadhi that she doesn't need any help from others.

Even as she witnesses Nanni's pride silently and smiles to herself, she begins to worry that she might never agree to sit on that filthy plastic chair. She recognizes that rather than anxiety it is a feeling of anticipation about what is to come.

When she chances to look at Raadhi's face, it

seems to have acquired a sudden glow. What could have brought such lustre to a face that was twisted in agony throughout the journey? Puzzled, she casts a glance around and, not finding anything, peers intently at Raadhi's face again.

Raadhi's gaze is flitting between the vacant seat next to her and Nanni. As Raadhi's anticipation becomes clear to her, she remains silent.

With both hands on her hips, Nanni looks around with an imperious air. Keen that Nanni must not become wise to their interest, she turns her attention nervously to the door of the doctor's room.

Nanni takes out the yellow cloth bag tucked under her arm. Her hand enters it and comes out; it holds a sheet of newspaper folded many times over. With trembling hands, Nanni unfolds and spreads the sheet on a chair a little away from them, and sits down happily. Though the oddness of what she has just done is noticed not only by the two of them but everyone in that reception hall, Nanni doesn't seem bothered at all. She calmly takes out her betel box and prepares to have a round.

She realizes that the feeling of dejection that she normally experienced in a hospital environment has become much more intense that day. The need to finish their work early so they can return home becomes more urgent.

'Why haven't they called you yet? I had fixed the appointment yesterday!' Chacha asks them before striding over quickly to the receptionist's desk. She waits for him to return. After exchanging a few words with the receptionist, he calls out to them, 'Um, let's go.' His voice brings her immense relief.

Unsure about which of the two women should be led in first, she looks to Chacha's face. His hand, extending towards Nanni, clears up her confusion.

As if she has been waiting only for this gesture, Nanni stands up immediately. She and Chacha lead Nanni to the doctor's room. The swagger in Nanni's gait seems especially intended to annoy Raadhi.

'It's only blood pressure. Medication should be enough,' the doctor says. When they thank him and walk out within a few minutes, they find Raadhi staring at them, her eyes boiling over with jealousy. Nanni's bearing has become even more stately, as if to flaunt her good health, as she returns to her chair.

Even after she and Nanni have come out, Chacha stays back with the doctor inside. They had planned to seek advice on Nanni's problems without her knowledge. But she isn't hopeful. She sees clearly that they can seek all manner of consultations and advice but the treatment will not be effective without the patient's co-operation. She waits for Raadhi to be called in.

The change in the doctor's expression as he examines Raadhi's swollen legs is worrying.

'First, give the patient's blood and urine samples for the tests. Once the results are out in the evening, we will decide on the treatment.' The doctor's words make it clear that, contrary to her hopes, her ordeal is not going to end soon.

'Go ahead. I'll be with you in a minute.' Chacha addresses both of them, but she senses a private message in his expression.

As they step out of the doctor's room, they are rudely scolded by a nurse: 'Why are you standing in the way?' She ignores her caustic tone and starts walking towards the pathology lab. But the nurse asks again, 'Going for tests, are you?' Furious at not receiving any response, she stalks away.

The ill temper and hostility evident in the nurse's tone evokes in her a bitter resentment. Even though she is quite used to the apathy of hospital nurses, it strikes her as an intolerable aggravation on this particular day.

The lab is very small. A girl is sitting on a wooden

bench beside the table. Her body is so thin that 'there was not a smidge of flesh to pinch.' Seeing them, she stands up, neither hurriedly nor slowly but with just the required degree of haste.

'Tests? Give me the chit,' she says.

The nurse's face is as dry as a paper flower. Her white uniform, brown from overuse, looks like it might turn yellow very soon. The girl motions to Raadhi to sit on the bench in front of her and prepares to begin her task.

Seated on the chair, Raadhi pulls up her sari to the knees to assess the degree of swelling in her thighs, jabbing at the flesh with her fingers. Instead of being exasperated at the long wait ahead, her face reflects a sense of relief that they are going to make Nanni wait along with them.

When they return to their seats after handing over Raadhi's blood and urine samples, Nanni greets them angrily.

'What's the matter? Aren't we starting yet?' Nanni's high-pitched screaming sends tremors of shock through the reception hall. With everyone focusing their attention on the three women, she feels humiliated. 'We will, shortly,' she tells Nanni. 'Give me your prescription first.'

'We've bought all the pills. First tell me, when

are we leaving? If I'd known that we were going to tarry like this, I wouldn't have come with you.' A childish petulance is visible on Nanni's face.

Enjoying her discomfiture, Raadhi asks calmly, 'Jassi, when do we expect to get the results, only in the evening?' After enquiring with an air of fake anxiety, she picks up her prayer beads and starts counting.

She moves away from there, looking for Chacha. She is afraid that if she lingers on, she might lash out at Nanni. She also remembers that Raadhi is patiently waiting for just that one ill-tempered word that she might hurl at Nanni.

'Ya Allah! For how much longer should I wait here? Why was I stupid enough to get trapped among all these bacteria and phenyl smells?' Waving both hands in the air, Nanni laments like someone bereaved. She ignores Nanni, heading towards the reception. Chacha, who is speaking to someone, comes over to her and says, 'Shall we go and have lunch? It's already half past twelve.' He looks exhausted.

The sun is beating down the length of that hospital compound. Human bustle and traffic has thinned by now. The doctor will leave in a few minutes. They have to wait until his return, she realizes, and is instantly seized by the anxiety of coping with Nanni's tantrums.

'All right. Let's go and eat,' Chacha's voice sounds feeble as he walks towards the car.

She returns once again to the spot where they are waiting. Nanni isn't whining anymore. She marvels at how quickly she has come to terms with the situation. Raadhi sits there proudly, with the confidence brought on by Nanni's jitters. The evident curiosity of the remaining patients embarrasses her. Impelled by a restless urge to get out of there immediately, she says, 'Come. Let's go and have lunch.'

'Lunch can wait. Tell me when we are going to reach home,' Nanni says with a scowl. Recalling how Raadhi is waiting for her to lose her temper with Nanni, she replies calmly, 'Later this evening.'

'I can't stand the stench in this hospital. I feel like fainting. Don't even want to swallow, my throat's run dry. Awful, awful,' Nanni pleads, weighed down by the sorrow of imminent defeat.

'All right, come and eat first. We'll see about the rest later.' Trusting her words, Nanni gets up and goes out of the room. Taking Raadhi's hand, she helps her stand up and brings her to the car.

Anxious that no problem should crop up during

lunch, she asks them: 'Do you want to go to the bathroom?'

'Bathroom? Here?' Nanni asks arrogantly. After silencing Nanni with a glare, she turns to Raadhi. 'What about you?'

Since Nanni's comment has belittled everyone who used that bathroom, Raadhi says, by way of protecting her own pride, 'I don't want to, either.' She looks at Raadhi in dismay before setting out alone.

'I need to wash my hands. Take me there,' Nanni says. She takes Nanni with her reluctantly. When they come back, the table is filled with items ordered for them.

As she sits down, wondering if that much food is really necessary, she notices that Raadhi has already started eating.

Raadhi eats like a child. The way she has filled her plate with all the food signals her anxiety that it might run out. With a steady gaze and a smile, she watches Raadhi devour chicken and fish without looking up from the table.

Meanwhile Nanni's face contorts in disgust, as though she is watching a repulsive animal. She takes out the newspaper from the bag under her arm, spreads it over her seat, and then sits down.

Serving just one ladle of rice on her plate, Nanni says, 'If they have curd, order some. I can mash the rice in it and drink it up.'

'Why aren't you eating any of this food?' she asks Nanni.

'Do you think I should eat such food at my age? How can I digest it? What will happen to my body?' The scorn in her voice is meant to insult Raadhi.

Nanni's heartless snobbery makes her feel sad.

Unmindful of the people around her, Raadhi keeps tucking in with gusto. She has forgotten that she was vomiting through all of yesterday. It would do her good if she at least remembers the long list of her ailments.

The unrest visible on Chacha's face after speaking privately with the doctor is weighing on her mind. Determined to extend their eating time somehow, she eats as slowly as possible. There is the danger of Nanni resuming her complaints as soon as they finish eating. Because of her anxiety about facing that ordeal, the food refuses to go down her throat.

Whereas Nanni has finished eating her curd rice in genteel fashion, it is strange to see Raadhi going at it with relentless enthusiasm. Unmindful of the fact that they are in a restaurant, Raadhi is sucking hard at each piece of bone.

It is past two when they set out from the restaurant. Nanni seems weary, as though she has decided that hurrying them isn't going to help anymore. She begins to hope that getting through the rest of the journey may not be all that stressful. The reception hall in the hospital is empty, with no patient in sight. On seeing them, the receptionist says, 'Big Doctor has asked you to collect the test results and see Junior Doctor immediately. It's urgent, he said.'

It is amusing how the receptionist's voice screeches like a rat with its tail caught in the door. She must surely have a nickname, she thinks, and wonders why she is having such thoughts now, unrelated to the time or place in any way. She makes Raadhi sit on a chair. Nanni has disappeared. What is she doing, standing outside? Oh, never mind what Nanni is doing, she tells herself, and makes her way to the pathology lab.

'Go and see the doctor alone. Don't take the patient along,' the girl in the pathology lab warns them. Her face looks even more wilted than it did that morning.

At the word 'alone', she pauses to think, and then walks back towards reception. Chacha and Nanni are asking the receptionist about some pills prescribed for her.

'Chacha, will you come with me for a minute?' she calls to him in a gentle, tension-filled voice and walks with him towards the doctor's room. From the way he seems uninfected with her anxiety, it is clear that he knows something.

When they come out of the doctor's room, they can't find Raadhi. 'Where has she gone?' she wonders, and looks around. Nanni's reply that Raadhi has gone to the bathroom takes her by surprise.

Nanni peers intently at her lifeless face, and then at Chacha. Determined that Nanni must not be allowed to infer anything, she averts her eyes and approaches Chacha. Swallowing the grief rising from the pit of her stomach, she says, 'Let's start immediately. After we reach home, discuss and come to a decision, we can come again tomorrow and admit her.'

Wanting desperately to find out more, Nanni scans both their faces by turns. Nanni's restless face also reflects the satisfaction of having discovered something. With dread gathering in the pit of her stomach, she goes to the bathroom in search of Raadhi.

The very thought of having to face the problems of the journey once again exhausts her. On the road, the faces of people on their way home in the evening look tired. It will be dark by the time they reach home. Raadhi is constantly mumbling something to her, and she responds by nodding absently. She feels like folding Raadhi's obese frame in a tight embrace.

To her son who asks diffidently if she wants the AC to be turned on, Raadhi says, 'Yes. Also play that cassette of devotional songs.'

She waits for those fingers to poke her waist. Raadhi's loud chatter and farts begin to fill the car. She is surprised that Nanni's fingers haven't jabbed her yet. She turns to look at Nanni. Her forehead is wrinkled in serious contemplation. She knows what Nanni might be thinking, but since it is impossible to stop her, she leans back peacefully and shuts her eyes. If her eyes were open, she would have had to witness the look of pity on Nanni's face. It is not something she needs right now.

Translated from 'Vilimbu'

The Trap

Long after I had fallen asleep, there is a light knock on the door.

I wake with a start. Who could it be? Suddenly I am nervous. I continue to sit there, reluctant to get up. I yearn for the person on the other side, whoever he may be, to go away.

The sound of knocking grows louder. I pretend that I am far away. With every passing second, I feel the knocks grow more urgent and the knocking hand closing in on me. The noise swells and spreads helter-skelter throughout the pitch-dark room.

I keep staring at the door, with absolutely no intention of opening it. When I can no longer put it off, I am overcome by fear. No one will knock on our door at midnight without good reason, just to chat about tomorrow's lunch or how the servant girl had not come in that day. Bad news is more than likely.

In the past, news delivered like this at midnight was always horrible, vitiating the atmosphere in our house. These days, just a simple knock on the door is enough to scare me. Staying awake night after night, waiting for a knock on the door, has turned into an unbearable ordeal.

Suddenly a light floods the whole room, disturbing my train of thought.

'Wretch! You're sitting here wide awake, and you won't open the door?'

He yells in anger because his sleep has been interrupted, and goes to open the door. Sleep is more important to him than anything else.

Each step he takes towards the door feels like a tremor inside me. Wonder what news awaits us on the other side! 'Ya Allah!' My heart whimpers and writhes in fear. I want to rush forward and grab his hand to stop him from opening the door.

He draws the latch back noisily, not caring that the child might wake up. I can hear someone from outside speaking to him in a soft tone. Unable to understand the low whisper, I try to listen with all my concentration. I crane my neck from the bed to sneak a look at the speaker. I imagine I can infer the news by merely looking at the face. His silhouette is hiding the person entirely from my view. I get up from the bed to ask him what the problem is. No matter how hard I try my body slumps back, drained of all strength.

I close my eyes, unable to bear the excitement, and pray to god. The news that will reach me in just a little while—who will it be about, what will it do to me? I recall the book I am halfway through. I remember Amma. How am I going to endure this? I see everyone's face flash before me and vanish instantly.

He steps out of the room. He is speaking to someone from the telephone in the hall. To whom, it is not clear. I feel suffocated, find it very difficult to breathe. My whole body seems to be roiling in fright.

Earlier messages had evoked fear rather than sorrow in me: a constant fear. Fear is a stronger emotion than grief. This message tonight could upturn everything in my world. Now he comes back into the room, picks his shirt off the hanger, puts it on and steps out.

'What is it?' I ask him urgently. My voice sounds very feeble.

Without turning towards me, he says, 'Nothing.'

He bolts the door from outside and walks away.

His reply is disdainful, as usual. His scorn has

always provoked me to anger or tears. But now, unlike in the past, I feel relieved. I feel strong, even. If the news was terrible, he wouldn't have been scornful. His reply even makes me happy.

That state of mind lasts barely a few seconds before another doubt surfaces in my mind. His 'nothing' could also signify protective concern. Did he say 'nothing' only because the news had to be hidden from me? If that were true, then…

Fear returns and clings to me again. I am close to breaking down. If I had looked at his face, there would have been no scope for confusion. Angry at my lapse, I scold myself.

If I had heard the voice, things would have been clear to some extent. My mind was focused not on learning the news but on avoiding it. My head aches. I hold my head tight with both hands.

I don't know what time it is. What's the use of knowing, anyway? The sound of a stray dog howling outside the window gives me the shivers. I am distraught when I recall that a howling dog is a bad omen. Hearing the dog howl, a few more dogs join in with fierce howls of their own. One by one, their separate howls meld into a relentless wail. I don't know where so many dogs could have come from.

There's no choice but to keep staring at the door till he comes back. My gaze refuses to remain steady. Why, why, why...the question seems to reverberate inside my skull.

Darkness has invaded everything. Suddenly, I feel as though I am inside a ramshackle cave. Like a fly trapped in a spider's web, I am gripped by fear and my body grows limp. My mouth is muttering repeatedly, 'Ya Allah! Save me.'

My body grows stiff from having sat still for so long in restless anxiety, and breaks into a sweat. I hear the sound of the room's door being opened. This is the moment when the mystery that surrounds me is going to dissolve. He comes into the room, unbuttoning his shirt.

He latches the door and goes to bed without saying anything. I turn on the light, wanting to hear the details. The darkness which had filled the room just a while ago disappears in an instant. He has closed his eyes in an attempt to go to sleep, and shouts angrily, 'You wretch! Don't spoil my sleep. Turn off the light.' Without a word, I switch off the light. Darkness, which was waiting outside, has crept into the room stealthily, without making a sound. It has spread itself above our heads, on the roof-beams, our bodies, and particularly his face. Darkness has a very strong appeal. It rests comfortably under my bed where no light can enter, and gazes at me.

I sit there wondering whether I should ask him or not. How long can I stay like this, gripped by fear and anxiety? I must of course face the consequences of unravelling the mystery—if not now, later! What am I going to achieve by deferring such knowledge until later? I feel as though the tension and fear are about to kill me.

'What's the matter? Where did you go?'

He abruptly turns to me.

'Won't you just drop it? I've told you it's nothing! Don't ask me unnecessary questions and plague the life out of me! How she nags all the time! Wretch!'

After yelling at me, he turns over and goes to sleep. The contempt in his voice is at its peak.

The peace that descends from somewhere brings me relief. 'Allah,' I mutter to myself. Since the anxiety is completely gone, I am feeling calmer. Fine, I don't have to feel afraid anymore. I can try to sleep. But the locked door frightens me. The street dogs' howling has not stopped yet.

Let the door stay open. For me to live unafraid, the door must be open. If this fear persists, I feel like I might go insane.

'Listen.'

I wake him. He is already fast asleep.

'What?' he asks in irritation.

'Why don't we keep the door open?' I suggest diffidently.

Uncomprehending, he asks, 'Why?'

'Just like that.'

'Why do you pester me like this in the middle of the night? If anyone comes to hear of this, they will spit on you. Can't you sleep with the door locked?'

After shouting at me, he goes back to sleep. I remain sitting there, and feel no urge to reply.

Translated from 'Pori'

The Curse

When she woke up with a start, she noticed that the sun had begun to cast shadows in the courtyard. Wondering what time it was, she turned her head sideways and glanced at the clock on the wall. It was close to six. I have to get up now, she thought. She hated waking up. Asleep, she could remain oblivious of time and memory; so she wished to snooze throughout the day. Still, she recognized that it was rare for sleep to actually come to her.

She forced herself to sit up. To be asleep during late afternoon prayer time was not proper. It was also the hour when the servants of God would appear. Moreover, people were likely to assume something unpleasant if they found her dozing at this twilight hour, so she willed herself to get up from the bed and walked to the courtyard.

As the sun's intensity dimmed, the stone tiles in the courtyard cooled a bit. It was impossible to set foot on these stones at noon, for they would be scalding hot. She remembered suddenly that Rashida, who had gone out in the morning, was not back yet. Shamim had no idea where she might have gone, or at whose doorstep she might be standing right now, begging for buttermilk. The very thought made Shamim's heart shrivel up in pain. As she reproached God for condemning Rashida to such misfortune, Shamim thought to rid herself of the drowsiness by washing her face, and approached the bronze cauldron in the courtyard.

The water, which filled the cauldron to the brim, looked beautiful. When she bent down to scoop some in her palms, the reflection of her face, with the evening sky in the background, cheered her up. Since the face that swayed in the water amused her, she stirred it with her hand and made it dance even faster. But what was the point of such play? She was overcome by bitterness, and felt dejected. How long must she go on, carrying the burden of this life? First, she wanted to be free of this thing that was weighing down on her family. Just as easily as she had shaken off the traces of sleep by washing her face, she wanted to be free from the symptoms of that burden that had spread all around her—and the affliction that had gripped her entire family. She yearned to somehow do away with the disease and its symptoms.

The sun had not completely disappeared yet. Ghani Chacha and Rashidakka would return home from different directions a little after sunset. She felt an itch on the back of her palm, and turned her hand to look at it. Because she had been sleeping on a rope-cot, the imprint of the rope was pressed into her skin. She rubbed it gently with the fingers of her other hand. Then she looked at her face in the chipped and faded mirror on the wall across the room. Though it was dim, her reflection gave her a lot of satisfaction. 'She has brown skin, but a radiant face'—she recalled what the women in her neighbourhood said about her. A lone strand of grey hair dancing in the breeze made her anxious. She caught hold of it, joined it together with the other strands and pushed it in. Remembering that she would turn twenty-seven in the month of Vaikasi this year, she sighed deeply. Nearly everyone in the village said with an air of finality, 'Why would she want to marry anymore?' They all spoke within her earshot. The fear that their prediction might come true tormented her constantly. She also remembered their mother, who had died soon after giving birth to her and her sister, Zeenat. The memory of her mother set off a yearning in her for a mother's love, bringing tears to her eyes. She wiped the trickle with the end of her sari and performed Olu, the ritual washing up in preparation for prayer. It was then that she remembered Radha.

After Olu, she shook out and spread the prayer mat on the floor, stood facing west and started to pray with the words, 'Mahrief's sunnaat', when her eyes suddenly fell on an old framed photograph on the table before her, leaning against the wall. Though she lowered her eyes and muttered the prayer chants, trying to avoid the photograph, she could not keep the memories related to it from rising to the surface of her mind.

'Um, do you know what all I remember when I look at this photo?' The words of the old woman from the 'gruel house', who had visited earlier that morning, sounded in her ears.

'Look at your Radha and Raadhi, just like a British overlord and his wife! Your grandparents lived in style, didn't they?' the old woman had said, adding in a tone of complaint: 'And then the Brahmin woman turned up to ruin it all!' When she remembered this, Shamim realized that her gaze had settled, in spite of herself, on the photograph and remained glued to it. Those two did indeed look handsome.

A few days ago, when she was trying to clear the cobwebs in the house, the pole had dislodged the picture-frame from its position on the wall; it fell down, shattering the glass. She had kept it on the table, planning to get a fresh piece of glass for the frame. Now termites had begun to gnaw at its corners. If she didn't keep it safe, they might gobble it up entirely, she thought, and felt a kind of animosity sprout in her heart. 'Yes, yes. I must definitely frame it and keep it safe,' she muttered wearily to herself. Even so, she imagined that Raadhi's penetrating eyes in the photo were peering intently at her. She stared right back.

Sayabu sat grandly in the photo, dressed in a white sarong and a full-sleeved shirt of the same colour. He was wearing a black hat on his head. A chain strung with gold buttons hung down the front of his shirt, proclaiming his status. The calm beauty of Raadhi's face as she stood timidly next to her husband reminded Shamim of her sister Zeenat. Jolted by the wave of unbearable anguish rising within her, she came back to the present.

Unhappy that these random thoughts had

distracted her during prayer, she focused her mind and began to chant again. Then she heard someone opening the front door. It was Rashida. She came in, sat beside Shamim and began to look up at her face steadily. Shamim was in a hurry to finish her prayers.

Her hair dishevelled and straggling in the wind, Rashida scratched her head noisily with the fingers of her left hand while pulling at the end of Shamim's sari. Sitting with her legs folded back under her, she said, 'I went through many streets today. Not one woman had buttermilk in the house. They'll surely go to ruin.' And in a spiteful gesture, she extended her hands in front and cracked the knuckles.

Shamim felt like crying when she saw Rashida. Once she finished her prayer, she flung away Rashida's hand that had been tugging at her sari, went to the kitchen, fetched buttermilk in a bowl, gave it to Rashida and asked her to drink. As she stared intensely at her, the fear that she too might end up like Rashida surged through her. But the very next instant she told herself that this could never happen, and found some solace.

Shamim wondered what would become of Ghani Chacha and Rashida if she got married and went away. It made her anxious. Shamim hoped that with her husband's help, they could get Rashida examined by a good doctor and get her cured. Even so, she felt dejected. As she closed her eyes and sat back on the prayer mat, she was gripped by the anxiety that she might have to remain a virgin forever. She picked up the Quran and began to chant.

Thoughts of Sayabu surfaced in her mind again. He spent all his time in the coconut grove, they said. If he left right after Bajru prayer to look after the coconut saplings planted by him, he would return only at night. He had no thoughts of home. A farmhand had to carry his food to the grove. 'He seems so proud going round and round that half acre of land!' Ayesha aunty would complain to one and all about her husband and feel delighted.

That evening, when there were clear signs that it was going to be dark early, with strong winds and heavy rain about to set in, he had walked to the road adjoining the grove with his friend Ismail and set out for the village on his bicycle. While darkness had descended on the hill that lay ahead, he could dimly make out two strangers approaching from the opposite direction. Sayabu and his friend stopped and waited for them to come closer.

A flash of lightning had revealed that the

approaching duo were a man and a woman. They observed that the woman was carrying a baby on her hip, and all three were thoroughly drenched.

'I'm hungry. Give me something to eat,' Rashida tugged at the free end of her sari. Shamim exhaled a deep sigh. Getting up without a word, she went to the kitchen, put some rice in a bowl and poured buttermilk over it. Then she opened the salt jar, picked a few crystals, tossed them in and mashed the lot. She brought pickle along in a small ladle and kept the food in front of Rashida. 'Eat without spilling on the floor. This is our prayer spot,' she said.

Rashida started eating ravenously, as though she hadn't set eyes on any food for days. In the way she sat and ate, she seemed like a child. Again, Shamim exhaled a long, hot sigh. She was overcome by fury against Sayabu for bringing this calamity on them.

Why had the couple come there at that late hour? Why had they asked Sayabu for a night's shelter from the rain? She was full of questions about that mysterious incident. She reproached herself for needlessly dwelling over them after so many years, but Sayabu's motive in letting the couple stay in his hut for the night provoked in her a deep revulsion for the man.

'It was the gold ornaments, glittering momentarily during flashes of lightning, which had set off the chain of events,' she muttered to herself, and suddenly her fury turned on that faceless woman. 'What had possessed that woman to wear so much jewellery when she was travelling? Cursed bitch!' she swore. When the jewels that had twinkled in the dazzle of lightning shone even brighter in the light of the chimney lamp inside the hut, Ismail's evil mind had noticed Sayabu's gaze transfixed on the woman.

After changing the child's dress, the woman laid her on the rope cot in a corner of the hut and sat there trying to press the warmth of her hands to the child's body. All of a sudden, she sensed Sayabu's hostile intent. She also realized that her husband, who had urged her from behind to go in and promised to follow shortly, had suddenly disappeared. She let her fear of not finding her husband pervade that dimly lit hut.

'Please let us go.' As she screamed, her words were drenched in fear, but that meant nothing to the two men. Everything had come to pass under the cover of the pouring rain. Finally, she had struggled all she could to make them spare at least the life of her child, but lost the battle.

Suddenly, unexpectedly, Rashida clutched and pulled at Shamim's hair. As she came to her senses with a wince, she forcefully extricated Rashida's hand away. Instead of making her angry, Rashida's prank merely evoked pity. 'What is it?' she asked.

'I am feeling sleepy. May I sleep?' Shamim felt a lump in her throat looking at this girl who was waiting for her permission.

'Yes. Go to sleep.' As soon as Shamim said these words, Rashida lay down on her lap. Shamim hugged Rashida with her right hand and stroked her back, imagining herself to be the girl's mother.

'It was Sayabu's friendship with that scoundrel that's led to all this, I'm telling you,' the old woman from the 'gruel house' would lay the entire responsibility on Ismail and curse him. 'But then, did that bald man have a wife or children? He was just an orphan. His sins went away with him. But who has been left to wander the streets now? That cursed fellow's company is the reason behind all this, isn't it? What can we say or do about it?' In her anguish, the old lady would have a crying spell in front of Shamim.

Realizing that it was the old woman's love and loyalty towards her grandfather and her family that made her talk in such a facile manner, Shamim quietly buried her own rancour in the depths of her heart.

Had Ghani Chacha not killed his wife by wringing her neck, Rashida would have received a mother's love. With that possibility ruled out, Shamim was saddled with the entire responsibility for Rashida. How was it fair? Shamim asked herself. With her open palms extended in supplication towards God, she asked Him the same question. She could not arrive at a definite answer. Pleading with God to give her at least a little strength of heart, she recited a few verses from the Quran and then looked down to blow on her chest. By chance her eyes fell on the gold chain around Rashida's neck, and the sight made her even more distraught and sad.

Rashida was so smitten with this chain that she would never remove it from her neck. Noticing that she was totally oblivious of it today, Shamim's heart grew weary with disappointment. Her elder sister Zeenat also had a similar obsession with jewellery. When nobody came forward to marry her, Zeenat had wept on her shoulder many times. Zeenat would open up to Shamim about everything, not minding at all that she was much younger. 'Why, Shamim, could it happen that I'll never get married?' She would ask this question time and again. Shamim felt that for Zeenat, the whole point of a wedding was to adorn herself with lots and lots of jewellery. 'When they make jewellery for my wedding, they should buy a stone-studded necklace and bangles in this design.' This was the only way Zeenat knew to nurture her dreams.

It was under these circumstances that Zeenat had to be married off to a boy who was a distant relation. His family was poorer than theirs by several notches. Though Zeenat was highly reluctant, there seemed to be no other option available to her.

Suddenly Shamim remembered the days when Zeenat used to wander around insane and out of her mind. Her eyes filled with tears. Zeenat had behaved just like Rashida did now. She would go from door to door, begging for buttermilk. And then one day, she disappeared altogether. Shamim asked a woman from the neighbouring house after much hesitation:

'Akka, why did she go around begging for buttermilk from every house?'

'Um, don't you know that the woman your grandfather had killed was from a Brahmin family? It's her curse that is stalking all of you, playing havoc with the whole family,' the woman told her, and went on: 'All right, so they were bent on killing her, but did they have to murder a blameless infant too and dump her in the well? Because they couldn't pull out her ring, they had chopped off the child's little finger. The wretched bastards.' As she ended her lament, the woman added, 'I was told the well was stuffed to the brim with the three corpses.'

Shamim sensed a strange emptiness forming rapidly in her stomach. Everyone at her home, known to the villagers as the mad Sayabu's household, was steeped in an inconsolable grief. Their situation became terrible only after the deterioration in Zeenat's mental state. After seeing what had happened to Zeenat, those who had thought until then that such things happened only to men started to wonder whether women too were susceptible to the same fate.

Unable to endure the burden of fatigue brought on by these memories, Shamim wanted to get up. After gently moving a sleeping Rashida's head from her lap and laying it on the floor, she stood up and waggled her legs vigorously. Fetching a pillow from her room, she lifted Rashida's head and placed it on the pillow. For a moment, she stared intently at the beautifully embroidered shapes of two parrots cooing to each other on the pillow cover. The realization that it was Rashida who had done the embroidery left her even more melancholy.

Shamim recalled that Rashida had been far more courageous and shrewder than her. 'She had knit more than a few wire baskets and embroideries by her own hand, after all,' Shamim marvelled, even as a mild patina of weariness unfurled over her face. Rashida had not been as dejected as Shamim by all the anxiety over Zeenat. She was still a woman who was capable of pursuing the few small hopes and opportunities that were available to her. Shamim, too, wanted to emulate Rashida's exemplary courage in her own life. Though both sisters were fearful of the grief that had settled on their lineage, they simply could not believe that it would weigh so heavily on their life and youth.

As the hopes she derived from appreciative comments from the neighbouring women—'Oh Rashida! She is such a smart girl!'—helped her pass the years, Rashida was confident that she was more clear-headed and independent than other girls her age, that the tragedy would not afflict her, and every misfortune would stand defeated by her intelligence. She spent most of her days proving this to herself and to others around her. Her talent for converting anything she could lay hands on into something useful for the household was beyond compare. Eventually the whole village was in awe of her, wondering where she had learnt all that she seemed to know. If she picked up a sheet of paper, there was a good chance that it would turn into a drawing or a paper box.

Keeping the accounts of milk sales stored in her memory, she could recall the amounts owed and tell her customers in the blink of an eye. In this way, she had helped to mitigate, at least partially, the severity of the curse that had been laid on her family. She nurtured the hope that some man would eventually seek her out—if not for her intelligence, then for her pretty looks—and instilled a similar hope in Shamim as well. When a young man from a neighbouring village turned up as if to make her dreams come true, she could still recall how the whole village was surprised.

Though Zeenat's ornaments were still intact, her parents sold them and bought new jewellery for Rashida. They matched the planetary configurations of both bride and groom, and avoiding the day of the week on which Zeenat's wedding was held, chose some other day instead.

'You should also be smart and brave like me. Then good things will happen to you.' These words of advice that Rashida had given Shamim just before leaving home still rang in her ears. Shamim remembered the glow of triumphant pride on Rashida's face and how it had enthralled her. She had also decided that only by following the path laid by Rashida could she free herself from all kinds of harm and nightly torments. While the whole village was waiting to see what would happen to Rashida, Shamim alone was hopeful that she would come to no harm.

Earlier once, while talking to her, their neighbour Zuneida had told her with much diffidence and concern, 'The girls in your family are perfectly fine until their marriage. Only after the string of black beads is tied around their necks do they become unhinged. That's why, even if someone comes along and proposes marriage, you should turn him down. I am telling you for your own good.' What she had said was indeed a hundred per cent true. It had happened the same way to both her sisters. She was very troubled by this. Once it was clear that nothing was in her hands anymore, she pushed aside everything she had learnt from Rashida. Overcome with fear that nothing could save her, she worried that there might not be any way out. Although the situation at home was such that she couldn't even dream of marriage, sometimes she was firm that she must not lose all hope. It was with this vestigial hope alive within her that she tried to get through her sleepless nights.

During those rare nights when sleep did come to her, dreams inevitably bloomed. Still, the bizarre notion that marriage could somehow transform her life's destiny eluded her grasp.

When someone slammed open the front door, Shamim turned with a start to see who it was. Ghani Chacha was entering the house. She found his appearance—unruly, matted hair and crumpled clothes—disturbing. After striding briskly towards her, he stared intently for a moment at the sleeping Rashida and then said, 'How about some food?' Without waiting for a reply, he skipped briskly over to the mat spread on the veranda and sat down on his haunches. Shamim remembered that Rashida, too, squatted just like him. A fleeting glimpse of his back made her wince. He must have walked through the slush somewhere in his slippers, his lungi and shirt had been sprayed at the back. Shamim felt weary.

'How am I going to wash these clothes?' she groaned in dismay as she got up and went to the kitchen. Scooping rice for him in a porcelain bowl, she added water and mashed it up. Before carrying it to him, she turned off the fluorescent light in the veranda and flicked on the night-lamp. Brightly lit until then, the room suddenly turned dark and was awash in the diffused light of the lamp. She went to the kitchen again, fetched the gruel in the bowl and kept it before him.

'Why did you turn off the light?' His voice sounded forlorn. 'How will I eat in the dark?' he asked as he started eating. She gazed at him with sympathy. She remembered how he would plead every time he drank the gruel, 'There is a finger in the gruel. Won't you please take it out first?' She consoled herself that at least no image of a child's finger being chopped off had formed in her mind yet. Sayabu, too, had kept screaming in his final days that there was a finger in his bowl of gruel. For some reason, her body shook and trembled. She wondered why she had to remember such things at this time of the night and frighten herself. In an apparent attempt to shake herself free of such thoughts, she shrugged her shoulders.

When she grasped with certainty that she was not going to sleep that night as well, she leaned wearily on the pillar in the hall. Deciding that she would spend the night being wide awake, she gazed fixedly at the bright moon glittering in the night sky that was visible from the courtyard.

An advertisement in the newspaper by a college professor in a nearby city announcing that he was looking for a second wife had excited her relatives. Eager to marry her off to him immediately, they quickly swung into action. Shamim was happy and satisfied that her hopes had not been in vain.

In order to ensure that the groom's people did not find out anything about Shamim's family history, her relatives went over to talk to the groom's family and finalized all arrangements. Shamim was disappointed, but realizing that she could do nothing about it, kept quiet. Learning that the groom had liked her photograph, she was relieved. She wanted to thank God daily for that happy event. Although she was bursting with eagerness to move from the first step to the next, she was also beset by worries about Ghani Chacha and Rashida.

Her relatives comforted her: 'We are here for you, aren't we? First, let this auspicious thing happen in your life.'

Initially, they had thought of selling Rashida's ornaments and procuring a new set for Shamim.

Then they decided that this might bring ill luck and dropped the idea. Leaving Rashida's jewellery untouched, they took up a collection among close family members and bought new jewellery with the money. They also bought new kitchen utensils for Shamim's dowry.

When she was alone, Shamim felt like laughing at the intensity of their concern for her. Was it only related to their zeal to get her married off? she often asked herself.

Shamim's relatives had decided that the wedding ceremony would also take place in the groom's house. They were apprehensive that allowing the groom's family to come over might lead to some last-minute hold-up of the wedding. Their precaution reassured Shamim as well. Before she was taken along with her relatives to the groom's village in a van, she was standing in the inner room of her house, crying over some random grievances from the past.

In the morning, after the nikah ceremony was over and they had enjoyed the wedding feast, the excited look on the faces of Shamim's relatives as they were about to leave the wedding hall frightened her enormously.

It's best that no thaali is ever tied around your neck.

As the voice of the woman from the neighbouring house sounded again in her ears, she held the string of black beads around her neck with trembling fingers. How could this object have the power to unhinge her mind? In despair, she smiled gently to herself. The fragrance of the rose garlands pervaded the room and made her dizzy, as she waited in tense anticipation of her husband's arrival. As soon as she had entered their house, it became clear that the groom's family was much more affluent than her own, and this filled her with dread. Wanting to shake free of it, she started wondering how old her husband must be. Since she was only able to catch a glimpse of him as he performed the wedding rites that morning, she guessed he must be forty-five and consoled herself that it wasn't all that old.

She inhaled deeply the fragrance of the rose, her favourite flower, and drew it within herself. As the sound of the door opening released her from the trance, she lifted her head to see who it was. Once she knew it was her husband, as if alive to the imperative that a newlywed bride must sit there passively, quiet and bashful, she lowered her head again. After stepping into the room and bolting the door, her husband saw her sitting on a mat on the floor. He made her get up and sit next to him on the cot. Though still shy, she sat down with pleasure. She had looked at herself in the mirror earlier to make sure that she was made up to look very pretty. With a lot of hope in her heart, she got ready to finally meet him.

Her husband had a calm demeanour. Though his complexion was quite dark, he didn't seem to be a rough sort. She liked him. She sensed within her heart the current of a vague anxiety that he, too, should like her. 'Have you had dinner?' His affectionate enquiry, accompanied by a friendly smile displaying white teeth, enhanced his appeal and made him even more attractive to her. She felt a surge of excitement.

Clearing his throat gently, he made another attempt to speak to her. She observed him trying to say something with great diffidence; she was prepared to listen.

He told her that after his wife passed away, he had had a very difficult time because no responsible person had been available to look after his four children and ailing father. He confessed that it was only to ensure that someone would attend to their needs and his own that he got married again. After a pause, he said, 'My mother is a mean woman. Because of her, no one was willing to give their daughter in marriage to me. Having no other option, I had to marry you in spite of your family being not so well off.'

'How does it all matter, anyway? There is no problem now. It's all for the best,' he said and exhaled a sigh. 'Now everything is your responsibility. My peace of mind is in your hands,' he said, sounding highly relieved.

Though she was listening to everything he said, she didn't open her mouth to speak. Instead, she looked down and nodded her head in a way that appeared to communicate her consent. She could easily detect the tone of newfound freedom in his voice. The impression that the room was overflowing with his voice, along with the sorrow it contained, troubled her deeply. She felt that the ease and comfort that had prevailed there just a short while earlier was gone entirely, and a tension had entered in its place. When she understood that he expected her to alleviate his sorrow, she was beset by confusion for the first time, but it soon became clear to her that it was no big deal.

Till the thaali is tied around your neck...When these words sounded again in her ears for some reason, she recalled that they had relentlessly stalked her since that morning. She decided that instead of frightening her, they made her laugh. However, she could not avoid her hands involuntarily reaching for her neck and stroking the black beads.

He took off his wristwatch and checked the time. Then keeping it on the low table next to her, he started unbuttoning his shirt. Contracting her body into herself from extreme shyness, she tried to shake off everything that had invaded and possessed her all this time. Releasing herself from all of it, she was getting ready with great excitement for her wedding night. She was going to experience for the first time a relationship that she had often dreamt of and staged in her imagination for so many years. She was also careful not to let him see her keen anticipation for a man's touch for the first time in her life.

With great effort, she tried to control her attention, which kept racing towards the rapture of that first instant when he would touch her, and her body, now aroused and adrift. When he started spreading over her as though sensing her yearning, she dissolved all the longing that had accumulated within her all these years and began to find relief.

When he moved away after working intensely on her, he broke the heavy silence that had ensued to ask, as though he had just remembered, 'How old are you?'

'Twenty-seven,' she replied, confused.

'Why was it not even slightly difficult for you?' he said, adding in a tone of vague anxiety, 'This was your first time, right?'

When he woke up at dawn the next day, he could sense a change in the room. He got up with a start and looked around. He saw her sitting in a corner with her hair open and dishevelled, a mess of broken bangles on the floor and loose flowers strewn all over. Frightened and trembling, he screamed, 'Come here, everybody!'

She continued to sit there, staring at the ceiling. The doctor who examined her said that she had been affected either by unbounded joy or extreme sorrow, gave her some medication and left. Her husband was puzzled, unable to understand whether she had been actually happy or sad the previous night. She got up, running her fingers through her hair which was hanging open and free, walked to the street in a hurry, stood at the doorstep of the opposite house and asked, 'Amma, give me a little buttermilk if you can spare some.'

Her whole body was fragrant with the smell of roses, her favourite flower.

Translated from 'Saabam'

Black Beads and Television

The colour television set that Shaukat Ali had brought home from Dubai was enough to make the whole village gape in open-mouthed wonder. Since there was no easy way to mount a rooftop antenna on his tile-roofed house, installing the TV had turned into a big problem for Shaukat. When he thought of going to Habib's house, which was two doors away, and asking whether he could fix the antenna on their terrace, Mahmuda dissuaded him. 'Aiyo, even if that man agrees, his wife Farida won't. The whole village is already envious of our television set,' she informed him.

This was true enough. It was midnight when Shaukat Ali had entered the village. If he arrived during the day, the whole street would gawk at the number of bags and boxes being unloaded, attracting the evil eye—Mahmuda had forewarned him in a letter. 'To avoid making everyone jealous, take a flight that will bring you home at night,' she had insisted during an urgent telephone call too. Just as she had feared, as soon as his car entered the village and stopped in front of their house, he realized that the lights had come on in two or three neighbouring houses and many pairs of eyes were staring at him.

When Hazrat from the opposite house, who was among those who called on him after the morning prayer, remarked, 'It seems you've brought home the devil too,' it was no great surprise for Shaukat. Shaukat knew that Hazrat could only regard a television set as the devil. He nodded without a word and smiled. When Syedamma from the neighbouring house told Mahmuda, 'Elei, it seems a whole lot of boxes were unloaded last night,' and laughed derisively, Mahmuda sensed her envy.

'A man who had left his wife and child behind for four years, didn't even know if they were dead or alive, worked day and night in scorching heat without proper food or water, has finally come home, and the wretched people in this village are so full of envy. May they lose everything they own.' While Mahmuda vented her anger at them by cursing without restraint, Shaukat Ali sat in silence on the pyol flanking the doorway of his house, not knowing where and how he might install the antenna.

'Instead of building a house with the money he's earned, he has lugged home a TV.' Amma's constant grumbling since that morning didn't fail to reach his ears. 'It's not as if I haven't earned money. It was an old TV lying in my room. If I bring it home, does she have to grumble so much?' Shaukat Ali muttered to himself. Proud of the distinction of being the first in the village to own a TV, he got up quickly and went out in the direction of the local bazaar. If he met Habib at his house and made his request, his wife might have a chance to intervene. So he decided to meet his neighbour in the market.

'What's the matter? You seem lost in thought.' Shaukat Ali looked up, startled to see Habib standing before him. 'Ada, may you live a hundred years. I was coming to see you,' Shaukat Ali held his neighbour's hand and greeted him.

'Is everything all right? Tell me,' said Habib.

'Nothing's the matter, really,' Shaukat said. 'I've brought a TV set. Only when the antenna is fixed high above the ground, the picture would be clear. The antenna consists of just three rods. Can I fix it on your terrace and run a cable to the set?'

'I see.' Habib pondered this for a while. 'No problem. You can fix it there. I am not going to stand there with an antenna on my head, am I?' Habib said with a laugh, before he dropped his voice and enquired, 'Are you sure that no thunderclap will hit the antenna, mapillai?' From his tone, Shaukat could sense Habib's anxiety about whether he had consented in haste and if his wife might scold him for it.

'Why would you even ask, machaan?' said Shaukat, worried that such irrational fears might induce Habib to withdraw his offer. 'You are a smart man, Habib, and yet you have such doubts. There are so many houses in the world with an antenna on top and here you are, asking me about it.'

Once he had been pronounced a smart man, Habib decided he could not turn down Shaukat's request. 'Oh…it's all right, then. You can fix it in my house,' he said, with an impassive expression on his face.

The worry about having consented without checking at home, and how he was going to appease his wife, was evident on Habib's face despite his calm demeanour. This caused some degree of discomfort, but Shaukat Ali got the job done without bothering much about his neighbour's predicament.

From Habib's terrace, Shaukat brought the cable down through the alley between the houses. He inserted it through a window in the flat-ceilinged extension of his tile-roofed house and placed the TV set at one end of the long veranda. The set received a solitary channel, in Hindi. Even then, if the wind was strong sometimes, there was no signal and only a jumble of dots appeared on the screen. If they were watching a programme at the time, they saw human figures for five minutes and only dots over the next five.

On top of everything, the language too was unfamiliar. Shaukat Ali was fed up. Did I bring this TV all the way here and go through all this trouble and humiliation only for this? he asked himself. He decided not to go anywhere near the set. Yet, his heart was overflowing with pride.

Though he felt this way, for his wife it was quite a different proposition. From six-thirty in the evening, women and children from all the houses in the street began to invade their house. Regardless of whether they understood the programmes or not, whether the picture was clear or not, the crowd did not get any smaller. Mahmuda, who in the initial days had proudly welcomed her relatives, served them tea and played hostess in general, started wondering why her husband had brought this wretched TV. When *Chitrahar* got over after eight and the crowd dispersed, she would grumble to her heart's content as she swept up the sand brought into the house by the visitors' feet. As far as she was concerned, the television had become a burden that outweighed their pride in it. Shaukat felt pity when he saw her doing these chores. Zakiramma from the neighbouring street was the only one who stayed back to help Mahmuda with cleaning the house.

Even if on occasion Mahmuda gave ten or twenty rupees cash in her hand, Zakiramma wouldn't accept it. 'No need,' she'd say. 'Don't I watch your TV for free? Then why should you pay me?' In the lone cinema theatre in their village, they changed the picture every week. Zakiramma would always be the first person at the opening show. She was fifty-eight and crazy about cinema.

Highly annoyed at her ways, her husband Sultan would vent his anger out loud. 'Look at her, thambi. Does it look proper when a woman of good family, a Muslim woman, loiters around? If there is an MGR film playing, she watches it every day. She is burning up all the money I earn by carrying loads,' he would protest.

'Yes. What about it? I'll go when I want to. I love MGR movies like my own life,' Zakiramma would reply.

'You whore...Gruel is all you eat and you want rosewater to rinse your mouth, do you?' Sultan would yell at her. Mahmuda and Shaukat Ali had to listen to their quarrels all the time. Mahmuda told her husband one day: 'Look at this Zakiramma wiping our TV set, see how lovingly she does it. The way she keeps patting it, I hope it doesn't get damaged in the process.' At times, she would follow Zakiramma on her way home, pick up some dirt from any spot trodden by her feet, mix it with salt and seven dried chillies, and along with twigs from the roof of their house, perform a ritual over Shaukat and the TV positioned next to each other, in order to ward off the evil eye.

'You have to do this too?' Shaukat would mutter to himself.

If Zakiramma had watched a film the previous night, she would, while cleaning the dirty dishes the next morning, narrate an elaborate analysis of the plot. The listener would feel as if they had seen the film themselves. Barring one or two women, no other woman went to the theatre to see films. No matter which film, Zakiramma would conclude her experience of watching it in a single word: laddu. All cinema was sweet and delectable to her. In her view, there was no such thing as a bad film.

One day, when Shaukat Ali happened to remark, 'That film was just no good. I also saw it yesterday,' Zakiramma retorted: 'Why, bhai, think about the amount of money they would have spent to make this film and how hard they must have worked. Is it fair that, after paying only 35 paise to watch it, we trash the film as garbage? That's why I will never say that a film is bad.' When Zakiramma said this while meticulously wiping the dust off the TV set, Shaukat Ali laughed, mostly to himself.

Mahmuda noticed that Zakiramma's eyes seemed to float in a dream-like state. At times, she would call out the old woman, saying, 'What's with the deep thought when you still have work to do?'

'It's nothing,' Zakiramma would say and resume her task.

Over the past fortnight, after Tamil programmes on Chennai Doordarshan began airing on their TV, Zakiramma rarely ever went home. She was unable to sleep a wink these days. 'Why should I go to the theatre to watch a film? Why can't I bring the film home, like in Mahmuda's house?' She began to dream.

'If television can be installed in a rich household, why can't it be put in mine, too?' she mused. The constant brooding began to hamper her work.

Her activities were reduced to passing her days in deep thought. All kinds of plans were being constantly worked over in her mind. Whenever her eyes, wrinkled from a lifetime of washing utensils, fell on the glossy smoothness of the television set, she was transported to delight and pleasure. She began to develop an intense disdain for her life without a TV. More than the lack of good clothes to wear, jewellery, a house or children, it was the lack of a TV that was eating into her. It was more pleasant to think of the TV as an essential rather than unnecessary item in the household. It seemed as though she had entirely forgotten that she was living with an old man called Sultan.

Since Zakiramma hadn't turned up for work till noon on that day, Mahmuda went to her house looking for her. She could hear Sultan's screams even from outside their home.

Since she knew that such quarrels were nothing unusual between the couple, Mahmuda pushed the tin door open and entered. The screech of the door's hinges drew Sultan's attention, which fell on her.

'Come in, Amma. Will you look at what this

woman has done?' In the corner where Sultan was pointing, she found a large television set next to a cardboard carton. 'Why do we need this? This useless woman has paid 4,000 rupees and bought it.'

Mahmuda blinked, unable to understand. A television set for four thousand rupees? How had Zakiramma come by so much money? She looked over at Zakiramma in confusion. She was seated majestically on a low wall abutting the kitchen. It seemed as though she hadn't heard a word of Sultan's outburst.

Zakiramma was gazing exultantly at the TV in front of her. Mahmuda thought that she might be wondering whom she could request for hosting the antenna.

'Do you know where the money came from? She sold her chain of golden beads. When I ask her, she says a string of plain black beads will do. Whom do I complain to about such travesty?'

Ignoring Sultan's fury, Zakiramma said, 'Why does he insist on hanging around my neck only as gold? What's wrong with plain black beads?'

Before her gratified desire, Sultan's wails came to nothing and faded away in the wind, even as Mahmuda watched in wonder and amazement.

Translated from 'Karugamani TV'

Toilets

There was a long queue waiting when they arrived. In the ambience and bustle of the hospital Shamim could recognize the hell she had seen in her imagination. After making a few comparisons, she reminded herself that all hospitals existed only to destroy human hope. She realized that instead of providing reassurance, they were intimidating. The shiny walls, spacious reception hall and the reek of medicine never failed, in one way or another, to trigger anxiety. She was older now, too. She noted that being middle-aged could well have caused this fear and anxiety.

One day two years ago, her cousin Nafisa's husband had taken ill and was admitted to a hospital. She had gone along with Nafisa's younger sister, Rafiqa, to visit him, and was seized by a mounting fear. Nafisa's brother told them that surgery was in progress and asked them to wait outside the operation theatre. As she sat there quaking, timidly holding Rafiqa's hands, sweat flowed profusely under her purdah. The fear that something untoward might happen held her as firmly as a prey trapped between an eagle's talons.

Scarcely conscious of the busy traffic of humans in that giant hospital, Shamim was praying silently, her mouth dry, when Rafiqa withdrew her fingers and moved away. Standing in a corner of the hospital's veranda, Rafiqa retrieved a small paper packet from inside her blouse. Emptying the powder from the packet on her palm, she rubbed it on her face.

Why did she need make-up right now, when her sister's husband was dying? Shamim stopped crying at once. Why should she carry the weight of an anxiety that Rafiqa herself found unnecessary? It struck her as odd that after Rafiqa came back and sat down beside her again, she started dealing with the nurses, doctors and patients' relatives with greater confidence.

'Next. Rajam, you can go in now.' Shamim found the harshness of the nurse's instruction, delivered as a command, irritating. The doctor had given them an appointment for noon. Seeing that it was past one now, she grew agitated. When she noticed the creases of pain on her aunt's face growing, she picked up her cellphone and called the doctor.

'Hello. Are you here already?' The doctor greeted her.

'Yes, sir. We've been waiting outside your room for a while now. My aunt's pain is getting worse. We wanted to come in, but the nurse wouldn't allow us.' Her grumbling tone must have embarrassed the doctor.

'All right, ma. You can come in now. I'll tell the nurse.' After disconnecting the call, she turned to her aunt. 'Please get up. Let's go in.' She led her to the doctor's room, gently supporting her with both hands.

When the nurse tried to stop them from entering the doctor's room on their own, Shamim pushed her hands away with a mix of impatience and arrogance. The look of extreme indignation on that girl's light-eyed, pale face was not enough to stop her. The woman-patient, who was in the room, stood up as soon as she saw them and, after seeking one last clarification from the doctor, strode past them on her way out.

'Oh, I completely forgot that you were here. What happened to you?' Though he enquired with his usual concern, there was regret in the doctor's eyes. Her aunt automatically sat down on the stool next to his table. The doctor placed the end of his stethoscope on her chest.

'I have severe pain in the lower abdomen, doctor,' her aunt said.

'Come, lie down…we'll see what it could be,' the doctor said reassuringly and led her to the examining table screened off from the rest of the room. The doctor had put on weight since their last visit. He looked roly-poly, like one of those obese comedians in Tamil films. As he walked past her, Shamim was amused by the sway of his buttocks.

'Since when are you having this stomach ache?' the doctor asked.

'From this morning, doctor.' When Shamim heard her reply, she was irritated. Her aunt continued: 'I boarded the bus at midnight and reached home only at seven in the morning. At around two I wanted to pee, but I felt too ashamed to ask the conductor to stop the bus. I've had this ache since then.'

'Why? How old are you—fifty-five, perhaps?' the doctor said. 'Why should you feel shy to say you want to pass urine? Why do you behave this way?' he questioned her aunt. There was a note of surprise in his voice.

'Come, get up,' he told her. Then he went near Shamim. 'You have to get some tests done. Shall I write a prescription?'

'Of course we'll get them done. Go ahead,' Shamim said. After fastening the petticoat over her bloated stomach, her aunt raised her sari and tucked it in at the waist. When she approached the doctor's desk and sat on the stool again, the doctor asked, 'Have your periods stopped completely?'

'My uterus was removed four years ago,' her aunt said.

After handing over the slip with the prescribed medical tests to her aunt, the doctor summoned the nurse who was standing by the door and said, 'Ask them to do all these tests. Then I'll prescribe the medication.' Shamim followed her aunt out of the doctor's room along with the nurse. By then, the queue of waiting patients had grown even longer. With anguish writ large on her face, her aunt walked behind the nurse.

Why would anyone suppress their urge to pee? As the doctor's voice sounded again in her ears, she remembered posing the same question to her aunt in a very harsh tone.

'I was feeling shy, ma. That's why I didn't tell anyone. How could I tell a bunch of men, "Stop the bus. I want to pee?" There was not a single woman in the entire bus.' Such was her aunt's artless reply.

Outside the lab, seeing a fully pregnant woman sitting next to her with belly out in front frightened her. She was surprised at how this fear gripped her whenever she saw a pregnant woman.

Once, when Shamim was seventeen, she had gone along when her mother was admitted in a city hospital for an operation to remove a cyst from her stomach. When the operation was over, her uncle was waiting to take Shamim back to the village. 'Why don't we let her stay with me for a few days?' Amma said.

Amma's words had made her unbearably happy. She pinched herself, unable to fathom the delightful prospect of staying outside her home for two days. She spent those two days in the proximity of Amma's agony, the wounds of patients in the adjacent rooms and the diverse smells of the hospital. She enjoyed the opportunity to chat with the duty doctors who came by to examine Amma, and with the young female nurses. She began to savour the way the young male doctor's curious gaze brushed her momentarily before moving on. On the third day, when her mother told her that she could go home, she was overcome by sorrow.

As the sad realization that she would never meet those doctors and nurses again dawned on her, she boarded the bus home with tears streaming from her eyes. She tormented herself with the foolish worry that the doctors might look for her the next day and find her gone. She put away safely, to no obvious purpose, the addresses of all the nurses that she had collected over the last three days.

'All the tests are done. The doctor will see you in the evening. For now, buy this medicine and give it to her. The pain will stop.' The nurse's voice released Shamim from her world of memories. The sense of comfort that follows relief from pain was evident on her aunt's face. They must have given her an injection of some sort. Feeling liberated since it was now time to leave the hospital, Shamim stood up in a hurry.

The car was scalding hot, having been left in the sun for a long time. Assailed all at once by the heat that eclipsed the air-conditioning, sweat, and the dizziness of hunger, she reclined in the back seat.

Regret for making Shamim wait for her in the hospital since morning was visible on the aunt's face. 'It took such a long time.'

When her aunt's murmur fell on her ears, Shamim nodded with her eyes closed. She felt that by agreeing with her, she could mitigate to some extent the guilt being experienced by the older woman.

She must have been sixteen then. 'Ah, ah, pull it up…pull it up…harder, that's it. Here, take it.' When she woke up startled by the melee of voices, she was confused, unable to grasp what was going on. Eyes still drowsy with sleep, she glanced at the clock. It was seven. Expecting a scolding from her mother for having missed the early morning prayer, she got up from the bed. Picking up the dupatta which had come loose, she stood near the bed and wore it properly. From the sounds drifting in from the backyard, she guessed that the motor was being repaired. She opened the window of her room and peeped out at the men who were standing in the stone-paved passage near the well. Kaliyappan and his co-workers were pulling out the pipe. Someone must be standing inside the well.

She had to pee urgently. She wanted to call out to her mother, but it seemed impossible. Beyond the stone-paved passage was the kitchen. She pondered for a while about what to do, then decided to raise her voice and call her mother. Her mother didn't like her yelling in front of men outside the family. Still, there was no other way out. 'Amma, Amma,' she called out in a loud voice. Feeling disheartened, she shouted a little more forcefully, 'Amma!'

'Amma, little sister is calling you.' Hearing her holler, Kali called out to her mother who was in the kitchen.

'What, you're up already?' As soon as her mother entered the room, Shamim said, 'I badly need to pee, Amma.'

'There are men standing near the well. You can't go there now. Hold it in for some time,' Amma said. The toilet in their house was on the opposite side of the courtyard, past the well in the middle. To get there, Shamim had to walk past those men. Amma was worried that they might see her.

'So what if they are standing? I'll rush there and come back. Or you can tell them to wait outside for a few minutes.'

'Why don't you keep quiet for some time?' Amma chastised her into silence. 'With two men pulling it from above and two more holding it from below, the job is only half-done. How can they let go of the pipe now? They'll take it out completely in a bit. Can't you wait for five or ten more minutes?' Amma pleaded with her.

'A girl should get up at five and say her prayer; this one sleeps till seven instead.' Amma complained, going on and on. Shamim clammed up and sat near her mother.

It was almost nine, but the work wasn't over yet. Sitting around without brushing her teeth was even more horrible. After waiting in silence for ten minutes, she repeated, 'I am going. I can't bear it anymore.'

But now a totally new idea occurred to her mother. 'Sit here. I'll be right back,' she said and strode quickly to the kitchen at the other end of the courtyard. She came back holding a wide, round plastic tub in her hands. Handing it to Shamim she said, 'Lock the door from inside and pee into it,' and went away. Shamim bolted the door, squatted over the tub and relieved herself. It felt as if she had come back to life after dying. Her mother carried the tub across and poured it down the toilet. Shamim remembered how she had suffered the same kind of acute pain in her stomach on that day.

Until she was eight, her family and her uncle's family lived in the same house. The sole cause of the daily rows that broke out between them was the common toilet situated in the back portion of the house. If they had to, for any reason, show their displeasure or retaliate against the other family, being the first person to enter the toilet in the morning or sending the boys in to waste time were oft-used tactics. Or they would empty all the water in the storage tub so that anyone who entered the toilet urgently would have to suffer without water to wash themselves. The skirmishes went on all the time, especially among the women of the household. Only later did her grandfather build a toilet in the stone-paved yard at the back of the house, despite the constant traffic of people there.

Abutting the entrance to the house was a toilet-cum-bathroom with a door covered by a tin sheet nailed to it; directly opposite was the well and the kitchen. Whenever people moved about in the courtyard or entered the house, it would be clearly audible to the person inside the toilet. Similarly, use of the toilet by women would become a difficult matter if there were men and visitors moving about in the house. When a woman peed, the patter of urine falling must not be heard outside. 'How can a girl make noise while peeing?' Amma would scold Shamim. Just to avoid this, Shamim would open the tap as soon as she entered the toilet for the noise of falling water. It would drown out the sound of peeing or shitting, making it inaudible to those outside.

When she had her monthly periods, the situation became even more horrible.

She had to wash and rinse her menstrual rag inside the cramped toilet, carry it to the room near the well at the entrance to the courtyard and hang it up to dry on the washing line. Odds and ends collected over many years were piled up in one corner of that room. On the other side, a heap of coconuts lay along with pieces of stripped coconut fibre. There was no dearth of bandicoots, centipedes and house lizards. She sensed with some alarm that the moment a light switch was turned on, they scurried away in every direction and hid themselves.

At times she had to walk past a cat that had just delivered a litter, growling at her from a corner, to hang the washed rag to dry as well as pick a dry one from the washing line to wear. She could not even imagine doing this during the night or when there was no electricity. Why can't we fix a washing line in a corner of the courtyard and hang at least one rag there? She couldn't ask her mother because she would say, 'The men folk might see it.'

She had to be lucky to be able to come out of the toilet immediately after washing and rinsing the menstrual rag. No man should be moving about in the house at that time. No one should see her as she crossed the distance of ten feet to the room with the rag hidden in her hand. For this reason, she and her sister visited the toilet only when there was no man present in the house.

On some days, if visitors, especially men, dropped by while she was washing her rags in the toilet, nothing could prove as horrible. Until her mother had chatted with them for at least half an hour, served him a cup of tea and sent him away, she had to remain standing inside even as her legs ached, sweating in the afternoon heat, and cursing the visitor, tears flowing from her eyes. A regular among the visitors was Amma's young cousin who wanted to marry Shamim's elder sister. He would come visit at least two days in a week, trying to catch a glimpse of his beloved on the pretext of speaking to their mother, incidentally boring her to death. As time passed, Shamim couldn't defecate out of shyness if people were moving about in the house, or if she heard them talking when she was in the toilet.

One day, she passed blood along with her stool. Amma immediately sent word for Saravanan, the doctor, to come on a house call. Feeling too shy to explain the problem when the doctor would inevitably ask her, she called Beeviyamma, an old woman, from the neighbouring house.

Beeviyamma arrived, walking on feeble legs and leaning on her cane for support. She was furious when she saw Shamim lying on the bed. 'Why have you fallen sick at this young age, girl, when you should be stepping on passing snakes?' After a bout of scolding, the old woman said, 'What's troubling you?'

Why has Amma invited this old hag here? Shamim was overcome with rage.

'Piles. There is a lot of bleeding when she is passing stool,' her mother replied. 'The doctor will be here soon. Please tell him. I'm feeling shy.'

As soon as her mother spoke these words, the doorbell rang. 'The doctor has come.' Beeviyamma muttered to herself as the doctor entered and stood in the hall. Pulling hurriedly at her head scarf, Amma welcomed and led him into Shamim's room. Shamim was mortified, cowering and shrinking into her body. 'She has piles, it seems. She bleeds while passing stool.' Beeviyamma's reply to the doctor's kind enquiry sounded disgusting even to Shamim.

'Hm,' the doctor nodded. 'Do you find something like a boil sticking out from where you shit?' he asked. That the question was being asked of her crushed her heart. How could Beeviyamma answer this question? 'Nothing like that,' Shamim mumbled, shaking her head urgently.

One day, when her uncle's daughter came home for the first time after her marriage to an out-of-town groom, Shamim's parents had invited the couple for a feast in their house. Shamim had been in high spirits since morning that day. After tidying up the house, she spread a brand new wire mat on the floor for the guests, placed the biriyani, chicken and other items on the dinner mats, then went to her room and sat beside her elder sister. She kept the window slightly ajar. She was curious about her new brother-in-law. Would he think that her family was indigent, looking at their ramshackle house? How would they manage if he wanted to visit the toilet? A thousand such worries crowded her mind.

The brother-in-law arrived with his family as soon as the evening prayer was over. Her mother's father and brother received them at the entrance and brought them inside.

From her vantage, Shamim could see her brother-in-law as he crossed the doorstep, passed the toilet and entered the hall. He was fair and handsome like Sivakumar, the film star. He wore a moustache. Shamim was crazy about Sivakumar. As a child, she had gone to a theatre twice and watched *Vellikkizhamai Viradham* (Friday austerities). Both times, she watched it only for the romantic pairing of Jayachitra with Sivakumar. She believed that they were actually man and wife, which made her happy.

A few days later, Shamim saw a news item in *Dinathanthi* announcing Sivakumar's marriage to a girl called Lakshmi. She was heartbroken. 'What will happen to Jayachitra, then?' she wondered. She was angry at that faceless girl, Lakshmi, because she had made Sivakumar break up with Jayachitra.

The brother-in-law was of elegant bearing and well-mannered. He spoke with tenderness to his wife. Akka—Shamim's cousin—dropped an English word every now and then, trying to show herself to be a bride fit for her husband. Though Akka had only studied up to eighth standard, Shamim had often seen her with the Rapidex book on spoken English by her bedside, studying it all the time. Her diligence didn't go in vain. Shamim resolved that very moment to buy a copy for herself and work on her English, and to marry a doctor as well.

From the day she set eyes on her brother-in-law, she began to dream of marrying a man just like him or someone even more educated. To ensure that her ignorance of English did not shatter that dream, she bought a copy of Rapidex and began to study it in earnest. When she had asked her brother to buy her a copy, he had mocked her with gusto.

'From now on your daughter will speak to you only in English. So you'd better learn English,' he told Amma and chortled. She was not in the mood to bother with his taunts. When the book reached her hands, she felt as though she was aloft in the sky. The doctor groom who visited her daily in her dreams harboured deep affection and love for her. He would bring her many presents. He was always full of appreciation for her.

She studied the Rapidex diligently and often rehearsed speaking in front of a mirror. 'Who understands English here?' she complained to herself. Dreams of the groom had begun to recur often. Her fiancé was sure to be dazzled by her intellect and English—and her beauty as well, she had no doubt.

She worried every now and then that her future groom might not like this toilet in the courtyard, with its tin door. What was worse, in the morning hours at least two or three persons each from the families of Savura, Tajira and Savuru would turn up with kudams, large pitchers, to collect water pumped by the motor in their house. It was her father's instruction that they be allowed to collect twenty kudams each. Since our poor neighbours don't have an electric motor at home, he had told his family, we have to provide them water.

In the mornings, these people would switch on the motor as though it was their own house, and collect the water that fell steadily into the tub. How could anyone visit the toilet during this period? None from her family did. What would they do if their doctor son-in-law had to go to the toilet in the morning? How was he going to put up with a toilet in the open veranda and the constant movement of people? She worried endlessly.

A couple of families with prospective grooms had come to meet her, then sent word that her family house was dilapidated, and it wouldn't be convenient for their son to stay when he came visiting. More than their refusal, it was the reason they gave that caused her severe heartburn.

'The girl is pretty, and we like the bridal gifts proposed and the extended family. But the house is in poor shape. How can my highly qualified son keep visiting a house that doesn't even have a proper toilet?'

'For any family function or festival, the in-laws must host the groom.' When she overheard their condition being relayed by Salam Chacha to her parents, she had to abandon her dream of a doctor husband, as also the Rapidex. It was not easy at all. She burst into sobs often. She felt angry at her family who, despite having a lot of assets and money, paid no thought to constructing a proper toilet.

Ever so often, she would vent her anger in various ways. When a house lizard or cockroach crawled up her leg in the kitchen, she would screech and shout with exaggerated fear. 'Why don't we knock down this wretched house and build a new one, like our uncle?' she would say pointedly.

At the time, Shamim's cousin was building a new house in the plot opposite their house. It was a three-storey building. Built with funds brought in from Saudi Arabia, it was coming up as a mammoth structure. That house subjected her to even greater torment. 'On all three floors of the house, there is an attached bathroom inside the bedroom, with fittings from Riyadh,' her mother said. Shamim had discovered the phrase, 'attached bathroom', with the aid of Rapidex. How wonderful it was to have a toilet inside the bedroom. It was beyond her imagination.

During evening hours, she would sit on the rope-cot in the courtyard, and gawk with keen interest at the new house standing tall before her. One day she wanted to see that magnificent bathroom for herself. They had finished plastering all the walls by then. Only the painting work was left. Whenever she thought about the colours in which they would paint the house, she would laugh to herself—as if it made any difference to her life.

One evening, when she was looking at an upper storey, she could sense that someone was staring intently at her. 'Who could it be? Even the labourers must have gone home before six,' she told herself. Someone was indeed staring at her, she concluded again, without a doubt this time. Not wanting to linger there, she moved from the courtyard to the veranda.

When Aunt Hajira came home that day for the night prayer, her mother noticed her muttering to herself and asked her: 'Why are you fretting and fuming?'

'Yes, it's those town boys who've come to lay mosaic tiles in the new house. They suck the life out of me, asking me all the time for water to drink. On this day of fasting, I feel wiped out.'

'Aren't they staying here? They must have asked you because you are their neighbour,' Amma said in a tone of disapproval that implied: why should anyone moan about giving water, of all things? At the same time, Shamim was excited by the news that some people might be staying on the top floor of the house under construction. When she was crossing the courtyard the following morning, her gaze involuntarily travelled to the top floor.

He was standing there, looking steadily at her. He was dressed in a pair of jeans and a T-shirt. Though of dusky complexion, he looked neat. She, too, looked at him. On realizing that her gazing at him was improper, she fled to the kitchen, stricken by shame and fear. From that day on, whenever she crossed the courtyard, she would always look at the mirror and adjust her dress.

She began to enjoy the thrill coursing through her entire body in those moments, when she espied a pair of eyes secretly watching her. She also grew to sense and crave that pair of eyes piercing her from mid-air, day and night, night and day.

Accurately reckoning the hours when there would be human presence on the upper and lower levels of that building, she planned her own activities to coincide with them. Planning her movements without being detected by anybody at home wasn't all that easy. She could walk about in the courtyard but she could not linger there without any apparent purpose. 'Why are you standing in the hot sun like a tree?' She would need to find a plausible answer for Amma's question. So she began to walk beyond the courtyard, between the kitchen and veranda. Her activities must appear to the young man as well as others in her house as natural. He should not think that she was walking around only to attract his attention.

One day, around seven in the evening, she saw him through the window in the soft light of that hour, talking to her friend and neighbour Fariza. She saw in his gaze at Fariza the same quality she had seen in his eager look that fell daily on her from the upper floor. After she could clearly see them holding a conversation made up only of signs and glances, she calmly moved away. Though a bit disappointed and sad, she experienced a sudden feeling of liberation.

For so many days, because she thought he might be watching her from the new building, she would visit the toilet only during the hours when she knew for certain that he would not be around. She realized with a sense of relief that there was no longer any need for such inhibition.

Every household in the village made arrangements to clean its septic tank once in two years. As soon as the date for breaking the tank was fixed, sorrow and anxiety would come to inhabit Shamim's mind. She would wonder if there were any means to make the day bearable, and torment herself. The day itself would pass without any hindrance. At around six in the evening, Singaram would come to her house along with his colleagues Murugan and Pazhani. Once she heard the doorbell, she would sit in her room and watch them. Sixteen-year-old Subramani, Singaram's elder son, would accompany them. His complexion was fairer than hers. Whenever she saw him, Amma would remark: 'Does he look like he comes from a scavenger's home? How fair and robust he looks, like a prince!'

Sometimes, Shamim would scold Singaram, 'Why won't you send this boy to school? Why do you bring him for this work?'

'It's all right, Amma. It's my vocation, what's wrong if my son does it too?' Upon hearing Singaram's reply, Shamim would be overcome with rage.

Singaram and his fellow workers would come at dusk and break the cover along the edges so that it could be lifted easily. They would break loose the lid of the septic tank embedded in the courtyard or backyard of a house and lift it, clean the tank all through the night, and fix the cement cover in place as before.

They would start their work only after ten, when all the windows in the house were tightly shut and everyone was fast asleep. The stench of shit would turn into an inexorable calamity, spreading through the entire street in waves. Even if she was in a room with all the doors and windows shut, under a heavy blanket, the stink would make it impossible for her to sleep. All night they would lift the shit out in buckets, pour it into the tall drums placed in a bullock cart and take it away. She would spend the night ruing the condition of Singaram and others. Amma would tell her, 'It's not as you might imagine. They start the work only after downing a few drinks. The smell won't affect them.'

Moreover, her aunt's house only had a dry latrine. During the same period, Singaram would bring a covered cart once every two days, pour the shit from her aunt's house into a bucket in his own cart. Then he placed a wide-mouthed steel bowl filled with sand in the latrine for their use the next day. His job over, he would move away, pushing the cart down the street, letting the stink of shit spread all over. Unable to bear the odour, she would run a long way from there. The stink did not fade that fast. When she heard one day that Singaram's son Subramani had died of brain fever, she wept secretly, without anyone knowing about it, feeling helpless in her distress.

Even in that moment of grief, she chose to vent her undying rage. 'Why don't we knock down this wretched house and build a new one?'

On their way back from the hospital, Shamim told her aunt about the urinary infection she had caught and explained how she must take the prescribed medication. 'From now on, if you want to pee, don't hold it in. It's nothing to feel shy about,' she advised her even as she felt like laughing at her own self. To this day, Shamim could neither understand nor accept how, with men present, a woman could ask them to stop a bus because she wanted to pee.

Shamim's biggest problem after marriage was not her husband, her mother-in-law or sister-in-law; it was the toilet. There was only one toilet in that house with eighteen residents. Even though it was newly constructed, it just had one toilet. It had spacious halls and seven-eight large rooms, but the toilet was near the back door, like a family ostracized from the village.

Regardless of whether she woke up at six or seven, she found that the toilet was always occupied by someone. To use it when she had to pee urgently was impossible. Until the person inside the toilet came out, she would stand a little away, in considerable distress—and invisible.

She found it impossible to rush in as soon as the person inside came out. There was no circulation of air inside. The lone window was really small and the smell was unbearable. Moreover, the floor was always wet. She hated going inside, but with no other option, she would fetch a plastic bucket filled with water and, standing a foot away, toss the water inside. Then she would wait on tenterhooks for ten minutes to let the stink fade away, with a prayer that no one else should turn up during that time.

Unfortunately, it often happened that some other resident did turn up during those ten minutes and barged into the toilet. Sometimes, if one of the boys or a man with a newspaper got in, her wait would extend to more than just a few minutes. And if by chance she managed to enter, the problem would take a different shape. If she heard the sound of footsteps indicating that someone was waiting outside, she would be unable to shit. She would think of how discreetly she herself had waited at a distance, without making a sound, and wonder with mounting irritation why this person was standing so close to the door.

There were many days when she would shut herself in her room and sob breathlessly over this problem. She would feel angry at her father-in-law who, in spite of his wealth, chose to construct only one toilet in his new house.

After this torment had lasted more than a few days and become a routine matter, she discovered a suitable time slot for herself: eleven in the forenoon. Boys and men in the house would have gone off to school and the shop, respectively. After that, when the movement of people slowed and the wet floor dried, she could defecate in peace. Since she had delayed shitting for so long, she had to shit again later, which often landed her in trouble. But how could she control the discharge during her monthly period? As soon as she got up in the morning, she had to go to the toilet, remove the heavy, soaked cloth, rinse it and replace it with another. Otherwise, the rag would get filled up and she ran the risk of stains on her petticoat and sari.

After entering the toilet in the morning and

rinsing the menstrual rag, she had to carry it in her hand while coming out. They had put up a separate washing line in the backyard where these cloths could be hung up to dry. When she came out, there would invariably be someone waiting to enter the toilet. Since it was the morning hour, it would always be men. It was inconceivable for her to encounter them with a wet menstrual rag in her hand. To avoid that difficulty, during such days she would take old copies of weekly magazines into the toilet. While coming out, she would place the wet rag between the magazines and walk away elegantly, as though with a stack of books. All this seemed reason enough for her to refuse to live in that house and go away.

She had gone to Kodaikanal once with her husband. This was the first time she saw an attached bathroom with a western-style commode. She exulted in the supreme convenience of having a toilet right inside her bedroom. However, she was not used to sitting on western-style commodes. Apprehensive whether it would work out for her, she met with failure on the very first day. The chief reason for the debacle: her husband was in the room, lying in bed. He was watching as she entered the toilet. He would have certainly thought that she might be taking a dump, she felt, and became inhibited. From the moment she sat on the toilet bowl, this was the only thought that occupied her mind. As a result, she was unable to defecate.

What kind of ordeal is this? Dispirited, she came out of the toilet. She calmed herself by thinking that it was a good thing she hadn't taken a dump, and became more relaxed. She decided she would use the toilet when her husband went out and waited for the moment he would go to buy cigarettes.

And as expected, he did go out. Immediately, she rushed into the toilet and tried to shit. But it is not possible to shit whenever we want, especially in a different type of commode. She realized this somewhat belatedly, and came out feeling dismayed.

During the three days they spent there, she reduced her intake of food to the point of starvation. If she ate heartily and didn't shit, she might break wind. If she farted with a bad odour, she was afraid that her husband might be revolted. She felt her stomach becoming bloated and heavy in those three days. Only after they got back home on the fourth day did she feel relieved. This time, the old, familiar toilet seemed superior to her.

Since there was a mindset that an attached toilet was an extravagance, and building one inside a bedroom would be an abomination, new houses were coming up without this amenity. The biggest cruelty of all was the agony she suffered during pregnancy.

After her belly started growing big, she suffered because she couldn't squat properly in the Indian-style commode. Generally, during pregnancy, the weight of the uterus presses down on the small intestine and creates blockages in the passage of faeces through the rectum, her doctor said, and prescribed tablets that she was asked to take regularly.

Squatting down with the weight of her distended belly and waiting for hours to pass stools was the most hellish experience of her entire life. She couldn't squat properly; so, whenever her legs ached, unable to bear the weight of her stomach, she had to spread the newspapers she carried on the floor in front and plant both palms on them to maintain balance. In the next ten minutes, her hands too would buckle under the weight and her whole body would begin to wobble. For washing herself, she could barely reach behind because her stomach was in the way; she experienced the ordeal every single time, every single day, as labour pain itself.

One day when she told the doctor about it, he was really surprised. 'Do you really mean to tell me there are no western-style toilets in your town?' he exclaimed. 'Why don't you build one immediately?' he suggested to her mother.

Because she had conceived twins, her stomach was really enormous. This could be due to excessive water retention or an abnormally heavy foetus, the doctor confirmed after a scan and sent her back.

On the way back in the car, she begged her mother: 'Please build a western-style toilet. I can't bear it anymore.'

'All of us were in your condition before delivering our babies. It's not as if no one in our town is giving birth. Don't fuss so much. Only three months are left for delivery, be patient. Why should we waste money building a toilet just for a few months?' Amma said and shut her up.

She had three children now. During pregnancy, the very thought of going to the toilet and suffering the physical ordeal while squatting down set off tremors in her body. She had to bear the burden of a heavy stomach from the fifth month. Whenever she met the women in her street who were pregnant, she would speak to them for a long time about her problem in the toilet and the agony. It became a never-ending story.

But these days, there were no houses without western toilets. After it came to pass that there were no women left in the village who didn't suffer from chronic knee pain, the Indian toilets in every house were knocked down and converted to the western style.

Whenever her elder sister who lived abroad visited with her husband and children, Shamim felt intolerably sad. The elegant manner in which her sister and her children conversed with one another in English set off pangs of intense jealousy in her.

She would describe their life abroad with its amenities and spotless elegance, making her relatives gape in wonder. She looked bright and radiant even now. While her cousins who were the same age looked withered like older women, she still looked like a modern young woman, bearing a faint resemblance to the film actor Sripriya. After seeing her, Shamim glanced frequently at her own image in the mirror and worried that her looks had declined with age. Her brother-in-law was handsome even today, and even more elegant than his wife. It didn't seem like he ever spoke to his wife in Tamil. They spoke fluent Arabic and English with each other. Now and then Shamim's sister would break into Urdu as well. As she had north Indians and Pakistanis as neighbours, she had also learnt Urdu. Her sister spoke a lot about the splendour of her imported kitchen and the cleanliness of her toilet. Over there, a person could lie down and sleep in the toilet, she said.

After seeing her sister's newfangled status, her husband's demeanour and polish, and the children's adorable looks, Shamim—instead of ruing her luck that had denied her such a splendid life—directed all her hatred and anger solely on the toilet with the tin door in her mother's old house. In the past ten years, there had been few opportunities for her enduring hatred against that toilet to subside.

As a child, Shamim used to spend the summer vacations in her grandmother's village. During those months, the village epitomized the very meaning of the word 'happiness' for her. She would start dreaming of the days she was going to spend there a full week ahead of her visit.

It was a tiny village. Though it offered Shamim many joys—like roaming around in the fields and the bank of the village tank, fishing in the tank with the boys from the neighbouring house, and learning to climb trees—there was not a single house in her grandmother's village that had a toilet. Her anxiety would begin early, during her bus journey to the place. It was an agony that obscured all the happiness she could experience there. Earlier, there was a dry latrine in her grandmother's house. It was the only house in the whole village that had a toilet. Grandfather was very proud of it, she was told. As in her mother's house, here too the toilet lay beyond the courtyard, a separate structure next to the flat-roofed room. Three of Shamim's aunts lived in the house along with her grandmother. However, since sundry household items had been dumped in that latrine, none of them used it.

She asked her grandmother if she could pee there. 'It is the only dry latrine in the village,' her grandmother said. 'There are no scavengers in the village to clean it. So we can't use it.'

At five in the morning or after eight at night, her aunts would walk past the village limits and head to Pettai. With a veil over their heads, they would trudge there furtively in the dark. They took her along.

Once there, they would find by the moonlight a spot along the foot trail running between the abundant cactus bushes growing on both sides and sit down to defecate. She would be frightened. Along with the buzz of fireflies flitting about, when the croaking of frogs and the drone of beetles fell on her ears, she would freeze in panic.

She was also afraid of encountering snakes on the trail. Moreover, when the stink of shit wrenched her stomach, she would feel like retching. In the moonlight she could see other girls squatting here and there on their haunches. For the first three days in the village, she would resolutely avoid going with her aunts to shit. On the fourth day, when she had no other option, she would join her aunts and set out.

In Pettai, when she walked among the cactus bushes and sat down behind a thicket, she would be so scared that some snake might sneak up on her from behind and sting her bare bottom that she simply sat there, unable to shit. When one of her aunts, after finishing her business, called out to her, 'Come on, let's go,' she would shyly say, 'I'm not done yet.' They would stand nearby telling her to hurry and get on with it.

Men who lived in huts in the fields had to cross the trail along the bank of the pond before they finished their business and went home. The women were in a hurry to get home before the men passed along that route.

Infected by their anxiety, Shamim would also get up when she was only half done and leave along with them. The worst experience of all was walking without washing up after a shit. Feeling the stickiness of the shit on her thighs, she would run headlong towards home. Once back, she would spend a long time drawing water from the well and cleaning herself.

When they received the news one day that Kalamma's husband had died, Shamim was in her native village. After waking her up early in the morning, Amma took her along on the trip to her grandmother's village. That night, after the funeral rites were over, Kalamma sat in the flat-ceilinged room, wearing a white sari and shorn of all jewels from her hands, feet and neck. When Kalamma's wails finally stopped, her grandmother said, 'Now she can't go to the village common. We have to find some way for her to relieve herself.' Extremely worried, Amma also agreed and sent for Saira.

When Saira came, Amma told her, 'Take the sand basket and go to the site where Rajangam from South Street is building a house. Bring river sand from there. Tell him I asked for some.'

'All right, akka,' Saira said. After she left with a cloth for the head and a basket, Shamim began to wonder. They had put up curtains all around Kalamma so that no one could see her. Amma was strict—no men, not even boys of Shamim's age, should set eyes on Kalamma.

When Saira returned, Amma asked her to dump the sand in the disused latrine a couple of feet beyond the well. Then she made Saira bring an iron plate from the inner room and asked her to put half the sand on the iron plate and place it in the latrine.

'I should ask our farmhand Marudhan to put a thatched roof over the latrine so that it is not open to the sky. I should also ask him bring the coconut fronds and stalks for it,' her grandmother told Amma. Then she put her arms around Kalamma and started weeping. Even after the house had been washed thoroughly, she felt that the fragrance of incense was lingering in every nook and corner. Until the end of the mourning period, Kalamma would have to defecate on that iron plate.

Though she wondered who would clean that plate, she didn't ask anyone about it. From the next day, before it was dawn the shit that Kalamma had excreted on the iron plate was thrown along with the sand into the waste basket, and Saira would carry it along with other rubbish to the village common and dump it there. Though she thought it was a neat arrangement, she didn't at all like that Saira aunty had to carry Kalamma's shit in a basket on her head.

When she asked for how much longer Kalamma

would shit inside the house, her mother replied, 'Another four months and ten days. After that she can go out.' Shamim was roused to pity when she thought of how Saira was going to carry Kalamma's shit through those four months.

One day when she was nine, Shamim was late as usual in leaving home for the madrasa. 'No, I won't go. Hazrat will beat me,' she stubbornly refused to go. But her mother was equally adamant in chasing her away. As she ran towards the madrasa, scarf tied tightly around the head and the Koran in her hand, the image of Ziauddin Hazrat that rose up in her mind threw her into a panic. A beating from him would be harsh, her hands and legs would be covered with red welts. Salam Azrat wouldn't beat her with such force. Not knowing what to do, she turned into the street where the mosque stood. It was deserted. Suddenly, an idea occurred to her. There was an alley behind Noor's petty shop, which hadn't opened yet.

Quickly, she dashed into the alley. She spotted a vacant space behind the shop, the size of a small room. There were a couple of stones and a thicket of plants and vines. A hen was digging for prey in the dirt. The place reeked of urine. It seemed like a spot where people relieved themselves in a hurry.

She was scared. If anyone saw her there, they would mock her as a loafer. If her mother came to know, she would ask, 'Did I comb your hair and send you off early in the morning for this?' and give Shamim a hard cuff on the head.

Yet, Shamim did not change her mind. Her class at the madrasa usually started at seven and ended at eight. It was already 7.15 when she left the house. The time now would be 7.25. She *had* to stand in that spot for another half hour, at least. Though her legs ached, she gritted her teeth and continued to stand there. The stink of urine gnawed at her insides. The hen looked up at her once, and then resumed pecking the dirt for prey. Except for the scraping of sandals as one or two people passed by, there was no other sound.

She shifted the weight of the Koran from one hand to the other. Exactly five minutes later, when she heard someone entering the alley, she froze in fear. A short, stocky man came in. Even as he walked in, he pushed aside the striped drawer under his lungi and held his penis in his hand. Seeing his organ, Shamim felt she was going to die.

The man must have been around forty-five. His face was puffed up and eyes bloodshot. His handlebar moustache gave her the fright of her life.

On seeing her, he pretended as though he too was shocked. But soon his gaze and actions indicated that when he entered the alley, he had been aware of her presence there. If he had come there to genuinely take a leak, he would have covered himself as soon as he saw her and left immediately.

Instead, standing very close to her, he held his penis in his hand and started stroking it up and down. She was disgusted by his behaviour. What a wretch! she thought to herself and hugged the Koran close to her chest. His gaze continued to traverse her entire body. The sight of his hairy penis, the hand that continued to stroke it and testicles hanging low and heavy made her feel like throwing up. She thought of fleeing from there. But he stood blocking the way. The idiyappam she had eaten that morning rose up to her throat.

Anxious that he might touch her, she started trembling. She didn't have the guts to close her eyes. He looked up and down at her as if to assess her appearance. She thought he might be wondering whose daughter she was. She wanted to shout her father's name and threaten the man that she would tell him, but the words stuck in her throat. The sound of children's footsteps started on the street. He closed his drawers and disappeared down the street.

She was overcome by a heaving urge to cry. She had no idea what to do, and waited until the last of the children had passed. If she came out now, they would see her. So she peeped out slowly when all the sounds had died down and after ensuring that no one was around, came out.

She reached home, hating herself for entering that alley without knowing it was used as a pissing spot, and feeling afraid of the sin that Allah would have added to her account for carrying the Koran there. Only after she had grown up did she realize what a dangerous situation she had faced on that day. Later, whenever she accompanied her aunts to the bushes during her holidays, the memory of that incident would return to her. Even today she trembled in fear that some man might come and stand near her in the dark. The fear and trembling she experienced every time she had to visit the toilet in the middle of the night during long train journeys was quite similar. That fear would stand before her like the sharp point of a dagger held against her throat or in front of her vagina.

Though she has used many types of toilets by now, they are still a source of terror in her life. On buses or trains, and inside airports or hospitals, most often she comes across only filthy, stinking toilets. During bus journeys, when the bus stops at a wayside eatery and she is told, 'The bus will halt here for ten minutes. If you want to use the restroom, you can do so now,' she would feel the need to pee just hearing those words. After visiting roadside toilets, she often had to spend the entire night trying to get over the disgust they induced in her.

Earlier, she used to wear churidar-kurta while travelling. But she began to doubt that this was the most convenient travel wear for women during the bus and train trips that followed. In restrooms she had to remove the churidar and squat down to pee. As a result, she contracted severe infections in her thighs and vagina, and suffered a great deal as a result. Later, she consulted a doctor. 'You should not undertake journeys, and if you do, avoid using public toilets,' he advised her.

Both were impossible for her. She discovered a third way: wearing a sari instead of a churidar. In the days that followed, the need for squatting in a toilet to pee did not arise. She even saw a few women pee while standing up. She began to follow this practice. If she had to pee, she would do it in a spot a little away from the toilet. Since there was no direct contact with the toilet, she could thus protect herself from infections. Hearing about this, Amma scolded her saying that it was not proper for women to pee standing up.

During train journeys, wearing a churidar made it easy for her to climb on to an upper berth for sleeping. But since she started wearing saris while travelling, she was unable to use an upper berth. She lied to the men in the adjacent middle and lower berths that she suffered from chronic knee pain and began to usurp their berths. She knew that if she confessed the real reason, the men were unlikely to help her.

Even when she was in a sari, she would never enter a train toilet if a man had just used it. Since it was one hundred per cent true that they would pee standing up and come away without flushing the toilet, she would wait and watch till a woman came out and go only after them.

This is how the great enmity between her and toilets endures even today. It's not an animus that can be ended easily.

Translated from 'Toilets'

Childhood

'Come in, marumavané. How are you?' Amma's voice from outside her room woke Mehrunnisa, who was only half asleep.

As she turned over in bed, wondering who the visitor might be, her mother called out from the hall, 'Mehru, come here immediately. Abu Tahir machaan has dropped by. Come, say salaam to him.'

Mehrunnisa was taken aback. Aiyo, it's Abu. When did he come here?

'Amma, why are you calling me?' she complained, and got up slowly.

She felt so giddy she could barely stand. Pain cut into her as if she was being hacked between the thighs with a sickle.

She stepped forward slowly, drawing the veil properly over her head, and stood in front of the mirror. Combing her hair back with her fingers, she tied it into a bun. Then she peered into the mirror again to check whether her face was bright or showed signs of fatigue. Her fair face looked anaemic, tired and pale. Even so, she realized, she looked beautiful. She applied some powder and lined her lower lids with mascara.

'What are you doing, ma? Hurry up, won't you? The boy is waiting here. Bring him something to eat.' She heard her mother calling out again.

The very idea of stepping out and standing in front of Abu made her feel shy. What would he think when he sees me? He might wonder, 'Why has she become so fat?' Ignoring the severe pain in her body, she came into the room, eager and ready to see him.

He was perched uncertainly on the edge of the sofa in the hall. When he greeted her with a friendly smile, she smiled back.

Abu was momentarily alarmed by Mariam, who ran to her mother and hugged her legs and Isam, who came crawling energetically on all fours, Amma noticed. As shame and humiliation ate into Mehrunissa, she smiled at him silently. She guessed that, like her mother, he too must have understood that there was no vigour in that smile.

'You are the same age as Meher. But she has a

child on her hip and another holding her hand. You were both born on the same day. Yet, you haven't even finished college!' Mehrunnisa wasn't sure whether it was joy or pride at having fulfilled her duty that she heard in her mother's voice.

For some reason, her discomfort was growing.

Meher recalled how she and Abu had played and studied together as children, and how she had coyly announced to her mother that she would only marry Abu machaan.

'How are you, Mehru?' He didn't like the way his aunt treated him as an adult. The way she kept calling him, a twenty-year-old, her son-in law made him squirm.

'Me? I'm fine.' Meher's terse reply rang out in a forlorn voice.

She was worried that he might already think of her as the mother of two children. She could have simply pretended to be asleep. But it was her eagerness to meet him that had drawn her out and made her stand before him.

'When do you finish college? Shall I bring you something to drink?' She was perplexed, not knowing what to say and how to say it.

'No need for all that,' he declined at once. 'This is the final year. Look at you. You've had two children…become a grown woman,' he laughed, staring intently at her as if in incredulous surprise and eyeing the children who were clinging to her legs.

'That's the way it is with a girl. They grow up in no time. Not for nothing do they say, "It's just one bleach for a new dhoti, one child for a young girl." They become old after that. *You* still look like a boy, though.' As Amma laughed, Meher felt anger bubbling up inside. Not knowing whether to laugh along with her, Abu looked around bewildered.

You are very beautiful, di. As she recalled Abu whispering in her ear when they were classmates in eighth standard, Meher stared intently at his face.

It seemed as though she was trying to guess what he was thinking, from his gaze. A failure to detect any change in his manner left her feeling like a defeated woman. He had grown quite tall and handsome. His blue shirt lent him a certain appeal. Oblivious of her own situation, she enjoyed his looks.

'Go ahead, ma. Go and bring him the tea. I'll mind the children.' Pulling both the kids clinging to Mehrunnisa's legs and fastening them to herself, Amma freed her.

'No, no. I have to go. I have a couple of friends

waiting outside. A friend's sister is getting married in a nearby town. We came here together. I'll take your leave,' he apologized urgently.

'Really? You should have asked them to come in. What a strange boy!' Amma rushed out, telling him off fondly, and brought his two friends inside.

A boy and a girl entered. Mehrunnisa greeted them with a wordless smile.

The girl looked stylish. She was wearing a beautiful black churidar. Her hair was arranged in a loose stack of layers. Though dusky, her face was glowing. In the couple of minutes after they entered and sat on the sofa, she had given Abu a searching look. Once she realized that a sudden fit of jealousy was taking shape in her mind, she consoled herself immediately with the fact that the girl was darker than her.

Still, standing there with her two children was humiliating, so she walked away in a hurry towards the kitchen.

As she set the water to boil for tea, she remembered the years when she had imagined Abu as her husband. Her mother had always called him son-in-law.

In those days, she couldn't pass a single day without seeing him. Since they were in the same class, she would always go to school with him. She would spend all her time at his house, which was in the neighbouring street.

Whenever she spoke to him she would use a few English words that Durai teacher had taught her, which she had learnt by rote. She would beautify herself, choosing with great care everything from clothes to cosmetics, just to look attractive for him. He would also perform many feats to impress her. After she turned thirteen and stopped going to school, she was forbidden from meeting him.

'Abu was in fact her traditional beau. Both were of the same age. We didn't get them married because we couldn't pair a first-born with another. Moreover, I was not in good health. We couldn't keep a girl at home for long, could we? So we married her off.'

Amma was prattling by herself. Mehrunnisa was furious. Why should Amma reveal all this to the visiting girl? With the anger that surged from her lower abdomen, she sensed blood flowing out and drenching her menstrual rag.

She felt dizzy.

'She is only twenty and this is her second abortion. And she has two children already! What's wrong with you people?' The angry words she heard yesterday from the lady doctor in town floated into her mind.

'He has no brains, sure. But what happened to yours? Who is suffering now?' The doctor's voice, blaring as she lay in a half-stupor in the operation theatre just before her abortion, still echoed, trapped inside her.

'What's the matter? Haven't you made the tea yet?' Amma, entering the kitchen with the baby on her hip, was taken aback seeing her daughter sitting listlessly on the grinding stone on the floor, her back against the wall.

'What happened, ma? Are you feeling faint?' Her mother rushed to her anxiously and shook her awake. Startled out of her reverie, Mehrunnisa said, 'No, Amma. I felt dizzy. Please filter the tea and give it to them.'

When the baby leapt away from Amma towards her, she pulled him into her arms and onto her lap. 'The doctor told you to keep away from water for four or five days. Why are you feeling faint? Are you bleeding a lot?' Amma asked her with concern.

'Yes, it's pouring out in thick blobs. The rag gets soaked fast. I can't keep changing it all the time,' she replied.

'All right, I'll send them off and be back,' Amma said.

She stared at her mother mixing the tea and adding sugar to it. When they had held marriage talks for her after she turned fifteen, she couldn't understand a thing. 'So, Abu is not the groom, is he?' she had asked her mother.

'Listen, girl. He is only fifteen. Boys don't get married off at that age. For marriage, he must be at least twenty-four. But we can't keep you at home till then, can we? A girl should be married off quickly,' Amma said.

She had no answer to this. 'Why such hurry for me?' she said again.

'You are a girl. How long can we wait with hot coals tied to our waist, kannu?'

For no good reason, they had dumped a boy who was born on the same day as her, studied in the same school, played together with her, and whom she had dreamed of as her husband, and got her married off to some other man. Had she too gone to college, she would have dressed as elegantly as that girl, isn't it? And perhaps she might not have got married yet, or had any childbirths or abortions?

To her, the very idea of entering the hall again was utterly shameful and humiliating. Would that girl think poorly of me, a girl with two children already? 'This Amma is an imbecile,' she groaned to herself. Where was the need to tell them my age? Idiot woman! She was able to see the sofa through the kitchen window. They were drinking the tea that Amma had offered. She found Abu's expressions disturbing.

That girl was sitting right across from him. 'Just two months left for the semester exam. I get worried when I think about Physics,' she was telling him. Had the girl spoken with an intimate lilt, or was this only her delusion? Meher felt a pang of hatred for the girl. As she eyed her neatly cut hair flying horizontally in the breeze, she patted her own well-oiled, tight braids in place.

'What did I tell you when you had come six months ago for an abortion? Didn't I ask you to use condoms?' The lady doctor's voice jarred her memory.

'We'll be leaving, then.' She heard his voice. 'Call Meher. I'll say bye to her before we set out.' But she had no wish to go out there. Quickly she laid the baby on her lap, unbuttoned her blouse and began to nurse the child.

Amma came into the room, looked at her and went away. 'Meher is feeding the baby,' she informed him. With great difficulty Meher suppressed the urge to see him again.

She wanted to be free of the memories from her past. As her lower abdomen and thighs grew heavy, the cutting pain came back. What would have been the gender of this foetus—boy or girl? she wondered. She could have kept it and lived peacefully, without feeling afraid, for almost a year. But now she had to face every single night with fear in her heart.

The baby's satiated smile and bouncing diverted her attention. She noticed that it was already nightfall.

'You should avoid handling water. Come and lie down. I'll wash the kettle and cups myself,' she heard her mother say. Her husband would be home in a short while. With the baby in her arms, she dragged her aching legs back towards her room.

Translated from 'Balyam'

Atonement

When Jameela woke with a start in the middle of the night and sat up, she found her body drenched in sweat. She opened her eyes wide at once and glanced around the room to check whether anyone was watching her. Her daughter and grandson were fast asleep. Darkness had enclosed the room like a heavy girdle. 'It was nothing, just a dream,' she told herself and prepared to go back to sleep. Still uncertain whether this explanation was actually convincing, she wiped her face with the free end of her sari and lay down facing the wall.

She closed her eyes, allowing the dream and the images she had just seen to surface again in her mind. Rashid was sitting on his heels on a prayer mat. When he looked intently at Jameela with his keen eyes as she entered the room, she was quite taken aback. She remembered at once that Rashid had passed away. Stricken with fear, she asked haltingly, 'When did you come?'

It was fear, not ardour, that had come to the fore.

But Rashid sat there in silence, still gazing steadily at her. She noticed the immense sorrow that lay shrouded in those eyes. 'Why have you forsaken me?'

As she inferred the question advancing towards her from those grieving eyes, she grew flustered and asked, 'Why? Why are you looking at me like that? What do you want? Talk to me.'

Her anxious tone evoked not a ripple of emotion on Rashid's face. He continued to peer at her tenderly with those gentle eyes.

'What's the matter? Why are you looking at me like that?' Her voice struck him once again, bounced off and fell to the ground. His gaze was unruffled, still set on her.

Jameela tried to urgently get away from the trail of her memories. Even after she was certain it had only been a dream, she found that her body was still trembling in fright. It was reality, after all—not illusion.

Just as a final tremor passes through a slaughtered hen, only a week before his death he had held on to both her hands and wept bitterly. 'I can't bear this pain. And I am making you suffer too much.'

Unable to endure the pain that stalked him, he had wept helpless tears many times over the past year. But not once had he cried out, 'Allah! This pain is unbearable. Give me death.' Jameela didn't know whether he could gauge the extent to which he was inhabited by an endless desire to live.

'It's not a good sign when the dead appear frequently in your dreams.' She remembered what the woman next door had told her that morning. 'They appear only when they realize that they might have left something behind.'

Jameela tried to rid herself of such thoughts. Recalling how deeply he had loved her, she wondered if that could be the reason why he appeared regularly in her dreams.

She remembered his boundless affection for her. She knew that it had been one of his life-goals to ensure that she did not suffer, that she was happy. Was that why he came looking for her, appearing over and over again in her dreams? Once she had thought of this possibility she couldn't abandon the idea, which made her feel miserable.

She needed a sleeping pill to get through the rest of the night.

'Should we send for the priest? We'll ask him to chant, and perhaps the dreams will stop.' She rejected her daughter's suggestion with a firm no. Whenever he appeared in her dreams, she sensed that his eyes were trying to convey something to her. She decided that she could not extricate herself from those dreams before she was clear about what that something might be.

He was in a bad way, clinging to a relationship that was only half over; to even think she could drive him away in that condition made her feel guilty.

Her children only had a limited understanding of their relationship, she consoled herself. Still, a sense of guilt engulfed her mind. She recalled how he had nurtured her with constant love and affection. She also believed, like others in her family, that she had indeed looked after him dutifully when he was ailing. So then why was he giving her such a sharp and pointed look?

As darkness began to fall at dusk, her children sat worried at her feet. She decided that she should never again say anything about their father appearing in her dreams and make them anxious. Besides, she didn't wish to give him a bad name in the eyes of others as someone who was still loitering around, not prepared even now to renounce worldly desires.

That night too, she began to wait for the dream. The fear that she had experienced during the preceding nights had vanished entirely. She heard a dog barking in the street. It had been many years since she had freed herself from the notion that a dog barked whenever it saw a ghost.

'What happened? Why are you sitting here wide awake instead of going to sleep?' His voice roused her from her reverie.

'When did you come?' she asked him hurriedly and looked in the direction of his voice. He was sitting in the same place she had seen him yesterday, and on all the other days, with the same demeanour.

'You spoke to me, didn't you?' she asked, surprised.

'Yes,' he said, as his eyes bored into her again. Wondering whether a look alone was enough to kill a person, she looked steadily back at him.

'I am worried whether I gave you any cause to be unhappy, machaan. Tell me if you had any complaints. Please tell me, for Allah's sake.'

Her hope that at least this gambit might elicit a reply from him turned out to be in vain.

'Remember? I used to cook rice gruel for you

and feed you little bits with a teaspoon. It pains me even now to think of how you had suffered, unable to swallow even that tiny morsel.'

Wanting to remind him indirectly of all she had done by way of tending to his needs, she checked closely for any change in his expression. His face remained impassive, calm and frozen. In the dimming light of the room, she observed that his gaze was still trained on her with a certain attitude, one that conveyed utmost pity.

Wondering what she could say again to break his silence, she ventured, 'When I keep thinking about you, I become ill. I feel dizzy every day. The doctor says it's just anxiety. Tell me, how could I not worry about you? Who should I think about, if not you? You used to be so strung out if I had just a mild headache…how can I forget that?'

Now that she had simultaneously conveyed her love for him and the affection he had shown her, she was at peace with herself.

Was he going to say something, at least now? She sharpened her ears and looked at him intently. She felt sad when he continued to be impassive. 'If you are still mad at me for not letting your mother live with us, I beg your forgiveness for that too. Please forgive me, for Allah's sake. Tell me, am I the only one responsible?

'Your mother used to give me so much grief when we were newly married. Afraid to bring home a sari for your beloved wife, you would post it as a parcel, as if my brother had sent it for me. You knew about your mother's quirks, didn't you? I am still haunted by memories of those early days. That's why I had resisted your proposal. When both your brothers, prompted by their wives, refused to keep your mother at home, why should I alone have carried the burden of looking after an aged mother-in-law?

'Even then, I am the one who recites the Fatiha every year to commemorate your mother's death. I've been doing it of my own volition, not because you told me to. It was perhaps to punish me that Allah had made you an invalid and forced me to collect your stool and urine every day.'

With a long, deep sigh, she tried to share those memories with him and at the same time, free herself from them. She gave up agonizing over whether he would show any signs of movement, or say anything at least now. Bitter and weary at the pointlessness of having bared her heart, she concluded, 'All right. Shall I go back to sleep?'

Every word she had spoken, she felt like it was all flying back at her like a ball hurled against a brick wall. For some inexplicable reason, she felt a deep anguish that made her want to weep bitter tears. Instead of putting an end to his visits by chanting the Fatiha like the others, she had wanted to ask him about his disaffection, resolve it and make him feel satisfied before sending him away. That he couldn't understand her intent left her feeling even more despondent.

She was confused about what to do next. 'Don't come here anymore. If dead persons appear before the living, it is believed that they have died with unresolved grievances in their heart and their worldly desires have not ceased yet. So, don't appear in anyone's dreams,' she wanted to tell him. But she didn't wish to hurt him either by saying such things.

All right, what did I do wrong? She wanted to ask him for the last time.

The howling of a dog from the street fell on her ears. She wondered if it was a pregnant dog howling from the agony of labour. Even a dog's cry seemed to magnify her grief. She knew of his love for animals. She couldn't recall a single day he had sat down to eat before feeding the street dogs. What had caused such silence and sorrow in him, she wondered in despair.

'Was I remiss on any count while taking care of you? I used to clean your body every day to keep flies and insects from bothering you. I collected and removed your stool and urine regularly. Did I ever wince in disgust? When you were ailing and infirm, did I ever bring up the matter of your infidelity with the intent to hurt you?' She wanted to tell him all that she had done to look after him, and rid him of his disaffection.

'Even on the day your soul departed, at around midnight, you shat on the bed in your sleep. I turned you over single-handedly, cleaned you and swabbed you with dettol. I did not wince even for a moment.'

As she was recounting the incident, the day of his death rose up in her memory. At once she remembered that she had wept copiously at the time. She also recalled that he had watched her tear-streaked face in the same manner as now, with a mix of keen attention and despair.

He had passed away that very night. When she realized that he had observed her teary face and the evident despair on it, she cried out, 'Ya, Allah!'

Then she suddenly turned in his direction. Not seeing him across from her, she scanned the room. When she sensed something grazing her leg, she looked down. He was crouched near her feet, in a posture of seeking forgiveness. There was nothing left except an immense silence.

Translated from 'Paava Mannipu'

The Orbit of Confusion

Dear Amma,

I am writing this letter to you, a woman who cannot read or write a single word, not just because I wish to, but also because I intend this to be an outlet for my growing anger towards you. This letter certainly won't reach your hands, nor will I ever send it to you in the first place. If a third person were to read it out to you because you cannot read it yourself, you might feel tremendously hurt and humiliated. It might also plunge you into endless agony. Since you are already suffering from heart disease and other complaints, this letter might, by adding to your stress, eventually kill you. I certainly don't want to make that mistake knowingly. Amma, you don't know how much I loved you, love you and want to love you. It's certainly not a love that can be captured in words.

First, I want to make one thing clear to you.

I am not, as you imagine, someone who has no love for you. I know that's what you think, and it has kept me awake many nights. How sad that a mother can believe that of her own daughter! Nevertheless, I am beginning to think that it may well be true. For the past few days, I've been wracked by fear that my love for you might be fading fast. A dreadful feeling that I might have actually started hating you, haunts me like a nightmare.

Why did I think of writing this letter to an illiterate like you? During this stressful time, when I can't share my sense of hurt and anger with anyone else or even communicate it directly to you, I am writing this letter only as a means of coping with my emotions. Certainly not to send it to you.

This letter is just like the one Kafka wrote to his father. There can always be many reasons for a father and son to be at loggerheads. So much of this is common knowledge. But a daughter is totally incapable of opposing her mother. This is true of all daughters and the reason is not such a secret. Girl children find it hard to hate a mother who is already being humiliated by their father. For them, it's simply unthinkable. Growing up in the constant company of their mothers, daughters see how oppressive the domestic spaces to which a mother is confined can become. They see their mothers wander listlessly, weep in despair, shrink from humiliation, and impound themselves within those spaces. Sometimes, daughters also witness the strange sight of their mothers marvelling at and admiring themselves. So I believed that daughters could not ever, at any time and in any situation, hate their mothers...till you turned Sharmila out of our house.

You don't know how I used to agonize whenever my father abused you and beat you up. His behaviour had given me all the motivation as well as the need to turn into a killer. I know that all the daily services you performed for him—by services, I don't just mean cooking meals, washing clothes and cleaning the house, but personal ministrations; such as removing the stalk from the betel leaves and preparing them for his consumption, washing his sandals and keeping them in the right place for him to wear the next day, cleaning and wiping his spectacles, keeping a small mirror, razor, soap and a mug of water ready on the front pyol for him to sit there and shave his face and beard. The list is very long. I also know that you performed these services not only because you were frightened of displeasing him, but also because you wanted to teach me something through them. My activities and behaviour, as also my tendency to contradict everyone around me, might have been reason enough for teaching me through your own example how a girl should behave with her husband. And so you wanted to instruct me in the art of being a good wife.

I couldn't be angry with you even if I wanted to. All I could feel was pity. I knew that the problem with you was simply the way you were brought up. You belonged to a family set-up that always followed and lived by the rule that a woman should obey her husband and family, perform all kinds of services and never talk back to anyone. So you could have been offended by the anger and resistance I displayed at times against my husband and brothers. That's why, considering the way you were brought up, I tried to reconcile myself to your behaviour.

Moreover, it was this society that had forced you to become the third wife of a man who was twice your age. I never hated you for wanting to live by the rules of this wretched society. I also imagined I could never hate you. But now, I am haunted by the fear that it could happen any day now. I started feeling this way only after you sent Sharmila away. Whenever I have felt intensely angry with you, I always remember how you toiled every day from morning to evening in our dingy, dark kitchen, starting from the moment you packed the stove with coal at the crack of dawn, to heat water in a cauldron. My rancour would instantly melt away. I would also remember those feasts hosted by Vappa for the holy men who helped him proclaim the intensity and pride of his faith, for which you had to work from morning to night in the kitchen, struggling with damp firewood, to prepare mountainous piles of idiyappams, mutton kurma and parathas. My compassion for you would flow like a wellspring.

You have spoken to me many times about your childhood years. Whenever I heard your stories, I used to cry for days. I was always aware that you indulged me quite a bit, because you didn't want me to suffer the terrible childhood that was your lot. Amma, you have told me how, since you were the first-born daughter in a household of thirteen children, your schoolbag was snatched from your hands and thrown away; about your mother, who, after every birth, handed over the responsibility of raising the child to you, ignoring the fact that you were a child yourself, and became pregnant again very soon thereafter; about your father who proclaimed that birthing children was a boon from Allah and prevention or abortion of pregnancy a sin.

You spoke also of roaming the streets carrying your siblings in your arms and on your hip, scarcely aware that you had been denied the very childhood that you were describing to me. You had no particular reason to tell me those stories, nor did you intend to evoke my sympathy. Even on other occasions, when you meant to tell me something else altogether, anecdotes about your childhood tumbled out involuntarily from your memory.

You reminisced often about your past in the form of funny, interesting and playful stories. You had entertained each child with specific tricks to get them to eat their food. Each child liked to play certain games. It was hard on you when some of the children came down with fever. At other times, they would fall down and come to you with bruises on their feet, arms and head, making your life even more difficult. Amid all this hectic activity, you had also learnt how to cook. Whenever children from your house fought with children in the neighbourhood, you had to go and appease their families. You had to overcome so many hurdles before you could drop your siblings to school every day. You also had to bribe them with toffees before leaving them there. And you had to cook food for the family along with all these chores…You invariably ended these reminiscences by complaining that none of them paid you any heed these days.

I am not qualified to feel sad that you had no proper childhood. My own was slightly better than yours, that's all. Otherwise, it was by no means enjoyable. What you wanted to give me was a pleasant childhood. But in this society, a mother cannot give her child whatever she wants—only society has that power. I know this. You know it well too.

Amma, how beautiful you are. Once, when you were cleaning fish, you called out my name and said, 'Look!' You wanted to show me a fingerling that was lodged inside the belly of a big snakehead. I looked at it, wide-eyed with wonder, and I still remember your face before me. Under brows that were truly shaped like an archer's bows, your wide, big, beautiful brown eyes. Oval face. Red lips. Amma, I would like to remember that face, childlike and beautiful, till the day I die.

It was your beauty that led me, many years later as a young woman, to compare myself to you and feel dejected before the mirror. I was neither as beautiful nor as fair as you. I grew up in a society which held that beauty and a fair complexion were essential for a girl. I had a slightly broad, square-jawed face, just like my father. Not a pretty face, by any account. Even a donkey looks beautiful in the prime of youth…I presented a fair appearance in a similar way. I knew that I wouldn't be as beautiful as you when I grew up. You knew it too. You even felt bad about it. That was why, whenever I came in from the street into the house, you would tell me, 'See how dark your face is. Wash it with soap and put on some face powder. Skin colour is important for a girl child.'

Before she turned eleven, every girl child in our community had her ears and nose pierced in a grand ceremony, followed by a feast and ceremonial gifts from her grandmother. When such a function was being arranged for me, you were very firm that your daughter shouldn't get her nose pierced. Though all the girls in our village had their noses pierced and wore nose studs and rings for many generations, you were adamant. Seeing all my girl-friends wearing nose-studs, I too was very keen to get my nose pierced. I lost my chance to wear a nose-ring only because you didn't want me to. I harboured regret and anger against you for many years. Whenever harsh and derisive comments were made about me for going around with a bare nose and allowing it to grow too hard for piercing, and about you for forcing it on me, I used to feel depressed.

But you never bothered about it. Years later, when I was grown up and mature enough to think for myself, you disclosed the reason to me. The face of a woman wearing a nose-stud is endowed with a special beauty. When it is removed after the death of her husband, the vacant spot robs the face of all lustre and the ornament that can never be worn again reminds her that she is a widow forever. I see that the nose-ring that I've never worn till today was shunned for a sound reason and I wish to thank you for it.

When our neighbour Farida's husband died a few days ago, her face without the nose-stud made me realize the harshness of her loss, and I felt relieved that this would never happen to me. You didn't burden me with the prospect of that vacant spot I would have had to wear if I lost my husband.

Do you remember, Amma, how crushed I felt

and wept inconsolably whenever you were subjected to Vappa's violent abuse? The countless number of mud utensils he smashed in his anger had been part of the dowry brought by his first wife. Those violent moments have played a part in determining how Annan treated his wife when he was angry, as well as my decision never to marry. Every time Vappa broke a mud pot in anger and walked away, it was left to you to search every nook and cranny in the house for any stray broken pieces and clean up the debris.

You were very particular about cooking Vappa's favourite dishes and preferred delicacies only when he was in the village. You wouldn't cook the sardines he disliked even if you and your children had a craving for them. Even if a procession of street hawkers passed our doorstep carrying basket after basket of sardines and we children begged you, you would not buy some and cook for us. Your entire life, you did only what pleased your husband.

You will certainly remember this. One day, I mentioned you and Father as the reason for my decision never to marry. You scolded me harshly. What do you know about the relationship between us, you snapped at me. It was definitely something you said only to soothe me. Neither of us was confused or sceptical about what I had said. But I did notice that you tried to conduct yourself very discreetly after that day.

If there was any situation that would make Vappa scold you, you took all necessary precautions to avoid it. For example, when Vappa entered the house, you were not expected to be praying or watching television. You were roundly abused if this happened. This was a regular occurrence and you had become used to it.

After the day I declined marriage forever, you avoided such situations with utmost care. I have no doubt that even Vappa was surprised by your behaviour in the days that followed. When he returned home, you were waiting for him at the doorstep. It was a drama enacted to remove all the distrust, hostility and suspicion that I had developed about the marital relationship. But you didn't realize that this drama put me off marriage even more.

Do you know why I am writing this letter to you? I am writing it because I am worried that my anger might turn into hatred, and my boundless love for you might begin to fade.

If my hatred grew or my love faded, I wouldn't even want to be alive, do you know that?

Though I have many questions to ask you, I stop myself because I am afraid that they might wound you.

I must have been ten at the time. A city-bred, educated woman of your age had arrived recently in our neighbour's home as the daughter-in-law. Feeling bored in the evenings, she made it a habit to come and sit in our house. I could see that her visits made you really nervous. She was not nearly as beautiful as you. I would always compare both of you and feel happy about it. But I never failed to notice that you were uncomfortable with the English words she let slip every now and then, the colours of the polish on her long nails and the well-starched cotton saris she wore.

Do you know something? Whenever she was there, you would pick up some weekly magazine and pretend to read it (though you merely gawked at the pictures) and it made me want to wreak vengeance on this society. May this society, which didn't even provide you basic education, go utterly to ruin, I swore.

Your nervousness seemed to confess that the lack of access to all such things in your village life was somehow your fault. Since she didn't even notice your discomfort, I wanted to stop her from coming to our house. But as a girl, I had no authority to stop her for such a reason. I knew that you protected me by not letting even the shadow of Vappa's aversion for girl children fall on me. I also knew that he never wanted to give me anything that he gave freely to his male children. But you didn't know that I knew. You believed that you had somehow compensated for that discrimination with your love. I also realized that I couldn't separate my father from a society which believed that only male children were valuable as heirs.

Though I can't say exactly when I began to lose my conviction that girl children would never have a conflict with their mothers, I think it has to be the day you yelled at Sharmila for no apparent reason.

She didn't know that you always wanted the men of the household to eat first (being your daughter, I was the sole exception). One day, when she stumbled upon me eating before Vappa and my brothers, she had her meal along with me because she was feeling hungry. And it made you really furious. For all that, her family was not of a lower status than ours. She was a girl like me, close to my age. All the privileges you granted me in our house, she also enjoyed in hers. She might have enjoyed a few more, but not less. You knew this. Even so,

I realized that as a mother-in-law, you would have expected her to behave like a daughter-in-law in our house. But the way you treated her and your hostility over a trivial issue—in my view, it *was* a trivial issue—was something new in you I had never encountered before. When I saw for the first time that there was another side to you that was harsh and cruel, I was frightened.

Once, when Ansari's mother failed to give me a share of the biriyani they had cooked for a feast in my in-laws' house, your anger knew no bounds. I am reminded of it right now. My mother-in-law had not done it deliberately. Since the number of guests that day had gone up unexpectedly, there wasn't enough biriyani left for the women of the household. But you saw this as a serious lapse and called my mother-in-law a low and despicable woman in front of my husband. You had transformed what I had casually shared with you into a grave problem. You should have seen the contempt on Ansari's face when he looked at me that day. I cringed horribly from the shame and humiliation. Since I had observed your gentle ways and how abominably my father treated you, I was indeed surprised at your conduct that day. But I also kept trying to see and understand it from a different perspective. Even so, every now and then, I would inevitably compare you with my mother-in-law and feel bad about it. Since it wasn't such a happy comparison, it left me feeling weary and dejected.

You were the one who forced me to compare my mother with my mother-in-law. Do you know how terrible I felt because of that?

Though Ansari tried his best to be a good husband, his drinking habit had created a rift between us. You had freely abused your own son-in-law at the time. Even if you didn't say anything to him directly, you never refrained from making unsavoury remarks obliquely, but always within his earshot. I knew that the underlying motive for your behaviour was the apprehension about your daughter's future. Even so, I never reduced Ansari's image to that of an evil man or someone who never loved me just because of his drinking habit. His love for me was immeasurable. He had never stopped doing things that would bring me joy. With or without his mother's knowledge, he would lovingly buy me many gifts. Whenever my sister-in-law tried to intervene or say something nasty, there were no comments at all from my mother-in-law. 'We were also like them at that age.' I was quite surprised that an illiterate village woman like her displayed such a wise attitude.

At that time, you had yet to attain the status of mother-in-law. So, there was no occasion to compare you with her. But today, I've become a seasoned expert in making these comparisons.

It was the day of Deepavali. When Ansari came home that night after a feast hosted by some of his Hindu friends where he had downed a few drinks, you wailed loudly in the courtyard for all to hear, that your daughter's life was ruined. Poor Ansari felt humiliated. It was yesterday's incident which reminded me of that day.

You know how weak your son, my brother, is when it comes to liquor. He had developed relations with some women labourers who came to work in his plantation, but you concealed those liaisons and arranged a marriage for him. You know those liaisons continue to this day. Nevertheless, whenever Sharmila had a row with Annan on the subject, you would say, 'Yes. He is a man and so he will keep straying. Don't make such a song-and-dance about it.' To top it all, you blamed your daughter-in-law in the matter.

I tried to understand your stance as a mother's reluctance to admit her son's shortcomings before a third person. I believed that it would dull the intensity of my resentment. Whenever I feel bitterness or hatred towards you, the only thing that can get me out of it is a memory of the childhood that you wanted to give me.

Dear Amma, do you remember how you tried in so many ways to sow bitterness in Annan about his wife by complaining about the thinness of her sari, about her leaving her head uncovered, about how she stood before the shop assistant boys and talked to them with powder and lipstick on her face? You had a critical opinion for every little thing she did and, in just one or two words, you managed to implant them in your son's head, almost as if in passing. Where did you learn to be so clever? I have never seen you try out any of these smart moves with Vappa. Were they hiding inside your head all these years? Though they surprise me every time, I look forward to them, always.

If you had shown even a little bit of this smartness while dealing with your husband, I would have been the first person to feel happy. But it was never to be.

My dislike or loveless attitude towards you is gradually taking on an ashen veneer, in the same way spoilt food items are covered by ash-coloured fungi.

Countless times I've watched helplessly as

you moved past all the betrayals your husband heaped on you, with only a faint tinge of bitterness. I expected at least some difference between the way you handled his oppressive behaviour, threats and insults and the way you moved on from his betrayals.

There was never any loving intimacy between you and Vappa. My brothers and I had always seen you servile before his domination. And for that reason, we always felt reinforced in our anger towards Vappa and love for you. Like you, we too had believed that a day would come when he would be more kind and patient with you. But even after our childhood and youth were over, that day never came.

We wished you would show your opposition to him in some manner, but it never happened. We expected you to express something like outrage or resistance. We were surprised that we couldn't see such emotions in you, though they come easily even to an average woman. We wondered about this for many years, with a sense of pity and regret for your plight.

But we didn't know then that you had indeed expressed your anger and retaliated against your husband. If we had known it then, what would your sons have thought about it and how would they have behaved with you? As for me, I would have been very happy.

It is true that after a long time, an incident today made me angry with you. I wouldn't say that this anger was born in a day. I understand it as something that was formed within me, in small, subtle ways, through a series of incidents over many different days.

Sharmila did all the household chores like an ox. You have yourself said 'like an ox' to me several times. There was only one problem though: she kept the house and kitchen as shabby and cluttered as a junk shop. She didn't know how to tidy up the spot there and then. I never considered it a major problem. I worked like that myself, and my mother-in-law would throw barbs at me now and then over it. But this was a gigantic problem for you. Whenever a visitor dropped in, you made it a point to lead them straight to the kitchen, point to its disorderly state and draw a comparison with yourself.

Do you know how such behaviour increased my distaste for you?

How did you have the heart to turn incidents in our house into exhibits for display to outsiders?

I really couldn't understand it. Why should the affairs in our kitchen circulate through the whole village?

I do understand that these humiliations you heaped on Sharmila as a mother-in-law were the result of the deep flaws in our family-centred social structure. I thought that there was nothing more in it for me to worry about.

But I would never want to intervene in such situations. If I was supportive of one person, I would incur the wrath of the other. Unfortunately, since the other person who was going to be hurt was you on most occasions, I chose to remain silent.

One day, Ansari and I had come by on a visit to our house. You had bought a lot of river fish because I liked it. Pilchard was a particular favourite. You sent Sharmila to the backyard to clean the fish. There you had fixed a stone slab on the ground with a water tap above, especially for rubbing and cleaning fish. Before Sharmila came to live in our house, you, Saramma and I would sit in the shade of the neem tree and clean the fish. That day, because Saramma hadn't come in to work, you asked Sharmila to do the job. Wearing a sour expression on her face, Sharmila turned abruptly and walked to the yard.

I, too, wanted to go with her to clean the fish. But I stayed put because I didn't want to upset you. Sharmila's scowling face made you really furious. You got up suddenly, walked to the garden and stood before Sharmila. 'Do you know who I am, the life I've lived and the status I enjoy? How dare you scowl at me?' you growled at her and came back.

I heard it too. I felt very bad. It was then that you heard Sharmila muttering something in reply and it fell on my ears too. Just one phrase: 'Oh yes, it's true that I don't really know your worth.' Since I didn't understand the subtext of this statement, I sat there feeling sad at the unpleasant exchange. But you were furious and shaken. I could see it in that moment.

Somehow I felt that the exchange between you and Sharmila happened in a language only the two of you could understand. In the days that followed, you began to employ all the tactics typical of a mother-in-law. I felt increasingly worried as I witnessed the escalating harshness of your manoeuvres.

You enlisted Annan, who was already disenchanted with his wife, in your battle. I wondered if you would have been so angry and full of hatred if Vappa had been alive.

If he were still alive, your entire attention would

have been forced to revolve around him. All your waking hours would be consumed by the effort to manage him and cope with his moods and demands. You wouldn't have an occasion or even a minute to complain about what your daughter-in-law was doing or not doing. Or, as you once said, the love and affection between you might have helped you both to guide and discipline each other in old age. Even now, the only entity I want to spit on and unleash vengeance on is this society itself.

How can you expect an old man who is twice your age to live with you till the end of your days? How is it even possible? Why shouldn't we spit on a society that doesn't even give a chance for that possibility to exist?

I was worried that the pressures you had to endure and the anger and contempt poured on you over a lifetime would turn you into an eccentric person. It's a worry that torments me even today.

Your weak muscles and creaking, swollen knee that glints like a waxed apple do not permit me to chastise you. I know how feeble your body and mind have become over the years. I witnessed their decline as I was growing up. I have seen you walk into a wide swath of paddy and briskly turn the grain over with your feet. It is not such an easy thing to do. My brother and I have seen you spin around, moving your feet effortlessly under a stack of paddy that was two feet high, and stir up the grain. We tried to do the same with our little feet and failed.

I have to accept that you have become weak before your time, like ten-year-old girls attaining puberty these days. In our time, we had to wait till thirteen or fourteen. Strangely, our women feel happy about girls attaining puberty at the age of ten because it's easy to get them married off early.

You, too, must accept premature ageing in the same spirit. One day last week, you went to attend a wedding in our locality. Since a daughter-in-law came to our house, you go out rarely.

If anyone told you, 'Now that there is a daughter-in-law in the house, you can leave her in charge of the house and visit a few places,' you would say, 'It's now that I feel like my feet are in chains. My daughter-in-law is not at all responsible, so I am taking care of everything in the house, including her.' You made a big fuss, as if someone picked up a whole house lying by the roadside and placed it on your shoulders. You had such a put-upon expression on your face.

When I saw your bluster that day, I was very

annoyed. You acted as though your house was as big as Buckingham Palace and there were a thousand things in it that you had to look after. All your words and actions seemed to turn on your fear that Sharmila should not take away any of the invaluable treasures piled up in there. Fortunately, I don't recall my own mother-in-law monitoring me in this absurd manner.

When you came back the other day from a betrothal ceremony in the neighbourhood, you had an impassive expression on your face for a long time. You looked totally lifeless. You appeared exhausted from your thoughts running helter-skelter in all directions. After a long period of silence, you said, 'Do you remember that educated daughter-in-law from our neighbour's house? She was at this betrothal ceremony today.'

No one in the village, including me, had seen her in a long time. You said, 'She is still as fresh and good-looking as she was in those days. There was not a strand of grey hair on her head as she entered, walking on sandals with slightly high heels.' From the way you emphasized those *slightly* high heels, you meant that she was no longer suffering from chronic knee pain and I should not think that she was wearing *really* high heels.

Though losing one's youth is an experience common to everyone, the recognition that someone your own age was in better shape than you certainly left you dispirited. I thought that the sense of regret you brought back from that encounter was excessive, as well as unnecessary. But I couldn't impose my opinion on you. I wouldn't want to, either.

You always wanted our house to be full of women from the neighbouring houses. You couldn't bear to be alone in that house. I didn't like you serving tea to women from all over the village, but you made Sharmila work in order to do this all the time. Usually, making tea for everyone in the house was Saramma's job. But you deliberately changed that after your daughter-in-law joined the household. It was a clever move because now you were able to show the visitors that you could command your daughter-in-law to do your bidding.

You ordered her to make tea separately for each of your guests. An unexpected outcome of this charade was that a few of your guests ended up telling you things that cut you to the quick.

'Your daughter-in-law is very beautiful, just like you. And she treats her mother-in-law as respectfully as you did when you were young.' They never said such things about me, your daughter. If they did, you would be over the moon. But when they had words of praise for your daughter-in-law, it seemed to fill you with bitterness and rage. I couldn't help wondering why. When you were already grieving that you had aged too soon, their words could only aggravate you further.

While you were still brooding that you had lost one-half of your son's complete affection, your hostility towards the young woman who was entitled to receive the other half too was so intense that it could not be gauged or understood by my tiny heart and brain.

One day you had gone to visit your cousin Said, who had returned from the Haj a few days earlier. When you came home, you left the gifts he had sent with you for the family—a box of dates, Zamzam holy water, prayer mat, cap, chanting bell and two black burqas—on the sofa and went away to wash up before the next prayer.

I was at my in-laws' that evening. By the time I visited our house the next day, a lot had happened in relation to the burqas. After seeing those two burqas, Annan had asked Sharmila to pick one for herself. Though both burqas were equally attractive, embedded with white and pale blue gemstones, one had extra work done around the neck, with plenty of embedded ornamental stones like a necklace. Like most women, Sharmila selected that one for herself.

Annan wasn't aware of the difference between the two burqas. Both were just burqas as far as he was concerned. I learnt later from Sharmila that the way you behaved and the vicious words you let fly after Annan left were simply beyond belief.

You had two issues. One, Annan had given her the right to choose; two, instead of leaving the better one for me, her sister-in-law, she had chosen it for herself.

Both were unacceptable to you, and you shouted at her for a long time. Amma, how can a burqa be good or bad? They are all the same, aren't they? My only fear is that such petty issues should not end up destroying the intimacy between us.

I have wandered for a long time in the muddy zone between loving you and hating you.

My problem is that I am able to infer the objective behind whatever you do. Once I've understood your calculations, I begin to wonder whether I can thwart your objective by performing other calculations to counter yours.

If you come to know that I have so many grievances against you, what would you think and how would you react? Will you be angry with me? Now and then, I do think along these lines. Though I certainly don't intend to send this letter to you, what if you come to know or find out by chance that my complaints and issues against you are so endless and so accurate? I wonder if you will hate me or get angry with me. No, certainly not angry. You might perhaps feel intolerably sad…but you won't rage at me.

Nor will you stop rubbing oil into my scalp once a week and stubbornly persuading me to eat regularly. Engaging yourself in activities that sustain me is an integral part of your life.

But you never had any expectation of developing the same kind of relationship with your sons.

For many years now, I have wanted to embrace and kiss you to express my love. Even though there have been many opportunities for realizing that wish, I have let them pass because I am too shy.

In our culture, we are not accustomed to embracing anyone except the husband to express our love. So I have never done this with you.

But I have embraced your mother and cried often as she lay unconscious in her final days. I have smelled the special odour of the elderly on her. But when I realize I have never once put my arms around you and held you, I feel ashamed.

I worry that there may not be any opportunities to do this in the future either, because I am afraid that my anger might come in the way.

I have silently witnessed the occasions when minor lapses like a lack of salt in the food, forgetting to bring back the salted pickle drying on the terrace before the rain, and less tamarind in the kuzhambu have turned into the equivalent of heinous murders.

Even if a coffee tumbler was left unwashed on the kitchen counter, your mental state would turn it into a horrible crime. Amma, I simply couldn't bear to witness your torment and agony.

This way of living has given you the neurosis of converting even trivial issues into gigantic problems. How to find a remedy for it is my main worry.

I know that it wouldn't be fair to fault you alone for this situation or to become angry with you. That's why I have changed myself and turned my anger into grievances against you.

I have seen you at work in the kitchen. You functioned in such a fine, elegant, smooth, subtle, measured and harmonious way, like a machine. Machines never grimace at anyone. Beyond everything, I also detected a certain pride in your face.

Countless years, making countless dosais, biriyanis, kurmas, idiyappams, idlis, parathas, chips, curries—even after having cooked so much, you exuded a relaxed sense of satisfaction. You could spend any number of hours toiling in the kitchen just for a few words of praise from someone.

While you never expected me to be as skilled and adept as you, it is so unfair that you expect it from your daughter-in-law, and feel disappointed. It's such a ridiculous expectation.

You saw Sharmila only as a thoughtless woman from a shabby family and found fault with her all the time. For some reason, she didn't seem to be very angry with you. She was truly thoughtless, perhaps. All she did was mutter to herself as usual. In her place, I would not have let you get away with it. My mother-in-law is much more reasonable than you. Unlike you, she didn't have to bring up ten younger siblings during her childhood. Unlike you, she had not been harassed and tormented by her husband throughout her life. This could also be the reason why she is far more amenable. By comparing both lives and balancing the arithmetic on both sides, I try to tone down my anger.

At some point that I cannot reckon precisely, your petty rage and the nature of your hatred morphed into a desire to drive her away.

Was it the time she said those words that day while cleaning the fish? I couldn't say. But you were adamant that she had to be thrown out of our house.

Although I sensed that there must have been something in those words that only you and she were privy to, I did not wish to speculate further.

But you were the prime mover. Sharmila was eventually driven out of our house as you wished.

Although Sharmila was thrown out for many reasons in addition to your intense hostility, only one reason was made public. It was broadcast all over the village that she could never have children. But only you knew the real reason why you had thrown her out. Your son was a naive man. You made him believe that missing or highly irregular monthly periods indicated the woman's barrenness. You told him that there were a few tests and treatments available for her condition and that she could get them done at her parents' home. Sharmila was sent away on such a pretext.

You could tell that story to the village, but you couldn't spin even a line of that yarn to me. How inconvenient it must be for you, I wonder. The house is filled with a vacuum that you created with your stories. That house in which you are living alone now brings you relief, as much as it makes me acutely uncomfortable. I am not crazy to be part of that empty space. There is little I can do other than going away from there, firmly suppressing my anger and grievances against you.

One day, both of us were sitting on the platform in the kitchen and talking about the village affairs. Your face was red and shiny like a ripe pomegranate. Fat jowls hanging down on both sides of your face marred the elegance of your features.

You asked Sharmila, 'Have they settled on a bride for your brother?' I had also heard the news from my mother-in-law. There was an urgent denial from Sharmila, accompanied by a vigorous shake of the head and the words: 'Oh, that! I believe they are talking to the other party, but nothing has been finalized as yet.'

This set off a fury in you like I had never seen before. 'Shut your mouth. I am their sambandi. How can your mother finalize anything secretly without consulting me? But you don't treat your mother-in-law with any sense of decorum or respect. Can I expect such things from you? Do I even need to? I'll ask around in the village and find out.

'It's my bad luck. I care nothing for your lot. Go away.'

I certainly didn't relish the power you sought to wield as their sambandi and the way you talked to her, as if your daughter-in-law's family didn't have the right to keep a private matter to themselves.

Enough, Amma. Through all these incidents I had to recall while writing this letter, I have reached an orbit of confusion in my mind. I have investigated and discovered a few solid reasons for being angry with you or hating you. Those reasons make me terribly anxious and fearful. I am afraid that this state of mind might do me serious harm. I am selfishly concerned that I must not lose your affection. It is out of this fear and anxiety that I choose to end this letter. If I don't do it now, I am afraid this unsent letter might stray from the endless grievances I've nursed against you and travel in a totally different direction. That direction could be one of anger, I tell myself.

I know that you might have serious complaints against me. I've challenged everything you've done, especially your treatment of Sharmila, but you have cleverly avoided betraying your feelings to me. Not inclined to respond to any of my questions, you turn your face away and wear an expression of contemptuous silence. Your silence can be truly distressing to me.

You know how irresponsibly I have often behaved at home. You would even say that I behaved 'like a young boy'. Your remark would always be tinged with a mix of pride and anxiety.

I have never picked up a household utensil without dropping it, and I have never handled any beverage without spilling it. Earlier, you never got angry about my clumsiness, but when you did later, I was able to face it. (I know that when I argued in support of Sharmila and because I criticized some of your actions, you tried to find fault with me.)

I am not uncertain about whether Sharmila will come back or not. I know that the doors have been shut against her return. If her periods don't become regular through treatment, there is no chance of her coming back. You are not a fool to allow something you don't want to happen. Yes, I realized recently that you are not as naive or foolish as I had thought.

There is only one problem, and I do think of it as a challenge.

Amma, I find myself at a point that can bring me the biggest sorrow of my life. I must not begin to hate you. The anger I have nursed against you must dissolve like the mists of snow.

These days, the confusion, hate, fear, despair, doubt, humiliation and anger roiling in my mind have enclosed upon me like a giant web revolving around me. Like a madwoman, I've been trapped by all kinds of anxieties. Your actions have demolished all the fortifications I had erected around myself.

In my mind I line up all the reasons—excuses, really—I have tried to invent to justify every action of yours, and to appease myself. Being truly farcical, they laugh derisively at me. Where can I fit those calculations designed just to deceive myself?

In the truths that grate on my mind, I experience, even today, many moments when I plunge into melancholy.

Like our doubts, our depressions are also profound. Moving past them is like going up a one-way street. I encounter mine, nearly always, in a helpless state. Like a nightmare stuck fast with glue in the depths of my mind, it refuses to leave me.

As usual, our family got together for the annual Ramzan feast. On our long dining table (which had come to us as part of Sharmila's dowry), an assortment of dishes, including mutton biriyani, fried chicken, sweet chutney and yoghurt khichdi, were arranged in rows. Before we took our seats at the table, I reminded myself that Sharmila had been present at the Ramzan feast for the last two years. Though she would have liked to be with her family for Ramzan, Annan did not allow her to go. She could leave only after the feast in our house. It wasn't a condition borne out of love. I know that you wanted her to help you with the household work. She knew it too.

This time, I was deeply embarrassed by her absence. The food refused to go down my throat.

No one else seemed to remember that a person called Sharmila had been present here earlier, or was troubled by her absence. I wasn't surprised, nor had I expected anyone to remember her. But it made me very sad.

That a person who was with us once is unfortunately not there today can make us very sad, but the fact that it didn't trouble you at all filled me with contempt and distaste.

I would never think lightly of the pain caused by someone's absence. This could perhaps be just my own problem. That I tend to think of it as others' problem as well must be due to my ignorance. But how could I think of you and my brother as outsiders? That man chased away his wife who had lived with him in the same house for four years, and was oblivious to her absence now. When I saw him, it brought my blood close to boiling point.

After throwing out someone who was an obedient maid helping with household responsibilities, you limp around carrying that burden along with your chronic knee-pain without appearing to be aggrieved or perturbed. I am really irked when I see you like that.

Dear mother, I am unable to understand what strange calculation prompted your decision to throw Sharmila out of the house. But I have absolutely no doubt that your decision was wrong.

These days, I remember Vappa quite often. I can't help feeling that had he been alive, he might have scolded you and Annan, and stopped you from sending Sharmila away. Since he always had to do something to neutralize anything you did, I believe he would not have allowed this to happen. You have created an opportunity for me to remember my father, a man I never liked very much. That the opportunity has been created because of you is very unfortunate for me.

I couldn't eat the Ramzan feast that day. The food wouldn't go down my throat. But you didn't see that. Since I sat down to eat with Ansari, you avoided being in the presence of your son-in-law. So you didn't know that I hadn't eaten properly.

Since Sharmila's family did not bother about all your efforts to show your authority as their sambandi, you were compelled to demonstrate your authority as mother-in-law and act in that horrible way.

The rancour you had accumulated over the years

like an ant gathering food bit by bit exploded one day. The words Sharmila aimed at you that day pushed you to the limits of your anger. Though I couldn't really understand or guess the meaning of those words, I couldn't accept them either, whatever they might have meant.

You cannot count on me for the support you need for the triumph you want so badly. You can celebrate Sharmila's ouster as the fulfilment of your wish, but it is very far from being a triumph. I would never want to accept a triumph forged on the defeat and pain of others. Just as I didn't accept the triumph of Vappa who tried to wield his power over you, I won't accept this either.

Dear Amma. You ensured that Sharmila too was subjected to the oppression you suffered in your own life. Since you are conscious of the violence that was your lot and know how it tastes, you should swallow and digest it completely. Don't ever think of giving it to anybody else. What you want to give is not a gift. The anger you faced, the violence unleashed on you, and the extreme neglect, must have pained you. How could it be fair if you wanted to give the same pain to someone else as a gift?

Simple people like us would like to share whatever comes our way (except material things, perhaps) with others. Love, anger, power, rejection—

we want to share much of what we have received with others. That's how I would like to understand all your actions.

I wonder if you have ever thought about the grief you've visited on your son, whom you claim to love more than your life. It is true that he doesn't have much love or concern for his wife, but you have never tried to ensure that he has a binding commitment in life.

Do you realize that you are behaving in a way that suits his irresponsible nature? You can't be oblivious to the void you've created in his life which will provoke him to even greater self-destruction, and lead him deeper into the mire of irresponsibility. Even more serious—I can't believe that hostilities and triumphs have become so important to you.

These days, you keep the anger you cannot unleash on anyone entirely to yourself, and nurse it inside you. One day, when I chanced on you fuming and muttering in our dingy kitchen, I was so deeply hurt that I broke down and wept.

When I unexpectedly ran into Sharmila last night, I was taken aback. I had gone to a nursing home to seek treatment for my fever. She too had come there with her ailing mother. When I moved closer with the intention of approaching her, she turned her face away as if to reject my gesture. I saw in her mother's eyes an expression of irrevocable hatred aimed at me.

They looked at me as though I was the culprit. When I thought about it, I had to accept that it might seem that way from their point of view.

They entered the doctor's chamber ahead of me and were about to leave the nursing home after their consultation. I wanted to follow them out but I hesitated for a few seconds. With a slight nod of her head, Sharmila invited me to follow them. I half-ran to catch up and stood directly before them. By now, we had moved from the nursing home entrance and onto the street.

Since it was eight in the evening, the street was dark. When I asked Sharmila, 'How are you?' it must have sounded like a sham greeting to her. She stood there, staring at my face. I could see the confusion and tension that hung between Sharmila and her mother, over which of them should respond to my greeting.

Sharmila spoke first. 'So, is your mother happy now? Ask her to sleep with her son, just as she slept with your uncle.'

The words that came leaping out of her mouth struck and knocked me down. When both of them walked off without looking back, I had to squat in the middle of the street. I needed a few minutes to realize that more than the anger in her words, it was what she said that had sunk me.

Amma, your loving daughter who has been distressed by her anger towards you wants, this day, this minute, to shower boundless affection on you. After getting rid of all my anger, I would like to take you in my arms and kiss you lovingly, passionately.

The affair that Sharmila used to insult you, that troubled you so much and prompted you to hide it from me, that you believed would make your children hate you if they came to know of it; for that one thing, because you had hit back at my father, because you had tried in your own small way to live your life in a society that had degraded your life, and above all, because you believe that you had done something wrong, I want to put my arms around you and fold you in a passionate embrace.

I have just one reason for embracing you despite all my complaints. Here I come, Amma, to hug you and kiss you. Before I do that, I am going to tear up this letter that I was never going to send you.

Translated from 'Kuzhapathin Sutrupathai'

Translator's Note

I first translated Salma's poems in 2004 as her contribution to a workshop for women writers from all over India. The translations provoked enough interest for an international portal for poetry to host more of Salma's poems in my translation, along with an interview and a few essays on her work. The poems, along with Salma's trailblazing first novel in Tamil, *Irandam Jamanglin Kathai* (2004), established her as an important new presence in the literary landscape. The publication of her novel in an English translation by Lakshmi Holmstrom, *The Hour Past Midnight* (2009), received wide attention from readers and critics everywhere. Following the novel, her collection of short stories, *Saabam*, was published in 2012.

It was after a few years of engagement with Salma's work as a translator of her poetry and occasional prose pieces that I started work on her short stories. Initially, I was to translate a selection of the stories in *Saabam*, but progress on this front was slow due to various reasons. In the meantime, Salma continued to write stories that were ambitious and compelling. These stories were more representative of the writer's growing mastery of form and structure.

And thus, we decided to include five of the later stories in this collection. Of the five, 'Karugamani TV' ('Black Beads and Television') was published in a festival edition of *Hindu Tamil Thisai*, and 'Kuzhappathin Sutruppadai' ('The Orbit of Confusion') was published in *Kalachuvadu* magazine. The other three—'Toilets', 'Atonement' and 'Childhood'—are being published here for the first time ever, in English translation. 'Pori' ('The Trap'), 'Vilimbu' ('On the Edge') and the title story, 'Saabam' ('The Curse'), are from the *Saabam* collection.

Earlier versions of 'The Trap', 'On the Edge' and 'The Orbit of Confusion' were published respectively in *Media Voice, Out of Print* and *Guftugu*. I wish to thank Asha Menon, Indira Chandrasekhar and Githa Hariharan for commissioning and featuring these stories in their magazines.

In both her poetry and fiction, Salma employs a direct and forceful style. As a writer, Salma closely follows the constant inner shifts of the women in her stories, who seem to be driven as much by memories and a wistful yearning as by the need to press on against a pervasive social condition of captivity and subordination. Her observation of the domestic world of 'ordinary' women is always subtle and rich in detail. The politics that Salma foregrounds through the personal tribulations of her characters has a universal quality to it. As translator, I have tried to replicate these layers of meaning in the translated text.

It has been a pleasure to work with Radhika Shenoy and Kartikeya Jain, my editors at Speaking Tiger, in bringing this book to its final shape. I acknowledge their contribution with gratitude.

N Kalyan Raman
Chennai
September 2020